I0831281

HELL 101

LOOK FOR THESE OTHER TITLES BY JOSEPH SWEET

FICTION

-THE DAMNED
COMING SOON

-DEAD TIME
COMING SOON

NOVELLAS

-THE INVASION

-I AM THE LIFE

NON FICTION

IN THE DARKNESS
2008

COLLECTIONS

-HELL 101

-THE FALL
2008

HELL 101

BY JOSEPH SWEET

ILLUSTRATED BY THE AUTHOR

Cover art and illustrations by Joseph P. Sweet

Photo by Azure Lee.

Digital work by Joseph P. Sweet

 All persons, places, and organizations mentioned herein, except those clearly in public domain, are fictitious. Any similarities to any persons, places, or organizations, living, dead, undead, or otherwise, is purely Coincidental. No trees were harmed during the making of this book... Oh, wait. Forget the part about the trees.

First Edition July 2007

Printed in the United States

Forsaken Press

http://www.forsakenpress.co.nr

forsakenpress@gmail.com

ISBN 978-0-6151-5939-3 (pbk.)

ISBN 978-0-6151-6387-1 (HC.)

Library of Congress Control Number: 2007907010

FOR AZURE.

AND TO CLAUDIA. WITHOUT WHOM, I'D PROBABLY BE IN JAIL, OR HAVE PUT A GUN TO MY HEAD LONG AGO.

TO BILL. WE MISS YOU BRO.

AND ALL THE OTHERS WHO ENCOURAGED ME ALONG THE WAY IN MY WRITING, ART AND MUSIC. YOU KNOW WHO YOU ARE.

"... AND THEY STAND
SO NEAR THE END
TIRED, YET FULL OF WONDER
CLAWING STILL
FOR ONE LAST BREATH
'FORE DEATH PULLS THEM UNDER ..."

THE DAMNATION CHRONICLES

CONTENTS

INTRODUCTION

Many people don't like to read this part of the book, or so I'm told. I put it in here anyway, because I myself have always enjoyed this part. Getting a little peek into the author's life, and why he or she writes.

For those who will skip forward, please do so. No hard feelings. I doubt I have anything of importance to say anyway.

More likely, this is just the ramblings of a guy who's happy to finally have the chance to ramble to someone in the front of a book.

I probably should talk about writing and the creative process, but I'm not going to. Frankly, I don't think I'm qualified with one published book to tell people about the craft. I'll leave that to the veterans. And it would probably be bull-shit anyway.

I will however, be finishing a book on self publishing soon, so watch for that. Once I found all of the information, I was shocked at how easy it was, and wanted to share that with others.

Depending on the success of this, I may also be doing an audio book version of Hell 101. So for all of you out there, who are reading this and would be interested in that, email me from the website at www.josephsweet.co.nr and voice your interest. Although it does occur to me now that if you're reading this, you probably aren't interested in an audio book version, but you might know someone who would be. So if that's the case, let me know.

I started writing when I was sixteen or seventeen. Constantly told by my step father, and others who should have been supportive and influential figures in my life, that it would get me nowhere. He said I should learn to do something real, before I ended up on the streets. Well, he was an asshole, and a control freak to boot, but I'll give him this. I have almost been homeless a few times. Luckily, the family members who did care, the ones who mattered anyway, helped me out when I needed it the most. The few people I would call friends have been there for me too.

It always seemed when I was down and out that there was someone there, picking me up and brushing me off. But no matter how much I wrote, or how many drawings I did, or pictures I took, or songs I wrote and played on my guitar, I never even made an attempt to become famous. I just loved doing it, and that was enough.

I'm still poor, and far from famous, so nothing has changed there, but it looks now like I may actually have a chance to live my dreams.

I'm also thirty, going on thirty one this year. Not exactly an old fart, but life is short and full of surprises, the biggest surprise of course, being death itself. I guess I just don't want to die with all of this stuff on a hard drive, or in my head, where no one will see it. And what's the point of writing it at all, if I don't get to share it with anyone? So I've decided to stop being selfish, and afraid of what people are going to say, and just put it out there.

Even if this ends up in the bargain bin at your local bookstore, and in a couple garage sales for ten cents, at least I know it's out there. That's good enough for me. Something I wrote will be out there in hardcover format, probably after we as a society are long gone. What good it will do then, I don't know, but it's something worth thinking about.

I go through jobs like most people change clothes, and the financial situation isn't usually great, but if one person reads this book, or the next one, (crossing fingers) and they like it, I'm happy, and it was all worth it. And all of those people who told me this wouldn't get me anywhere were missing the point. I don't need it to *get me anywhere.* I just need to do it. Everything else will work itself out in good time.

If you read this, thanks for letting me ramble, and I hope you enjoy the stories. More will come soon.

Joseph Sweet

FOREWORD

Hell 101 is a collection of short stories, spanning probably 14 or 15 years of my life. I wrote it because I had to. I have a very over-active imagination. More so when I sleep than at any other time.

I write down any dreams that I think could be stories.

Many of them are so vivid they don't even need fleshing out. I'll let the stories speak for themselves, as rambling about how they were written, and why won't help and may ruin them for you.

I think I decided that I wanted to be a writer when I was about Eleven or twelve. I had been in a really bad accident, and in a coma for a week. I started reading books not long after. That's when I read my first Stephen King novel, and was blown away at the thought which must have gone into such a thing.

I've read many books by many authors now, among my favorites are Jack London, Stephen King, Dean Koontz, some Anne Rice. Many other authors as well, but there just isn't time or room to write them all down. I started trying to write at the age of eleven or twelve, but quickly decided that I wasn't ready. I didn't try again until I was around sixteen or so, when my mother gave me an ancient looking - and very heavy - typewriter. We'll forget about those stories though. They weren't that good, and hopefully nobody ever sees any of them. There are a couple that may have potential, after a long hard rewrite, however.

All of these stories except one, especially the title one, are based on dreams I had. Some would call a few of them nightmares. These were the ones that stayed with me after awakening, and wouldn't let up. Eventually I found myself adding a text file to my USB drive, and not long after that I was writing and finishing them as completed stories.

One of them, "Just like going to sleep," I found in a notebook full of stories that I had written when I was still in high school. This is the only exception. I didn't dream it, I was just inspired to write it. Most likely, while bored in some class, attempting to keep myself from falling asleep. Very little was changed in that one from the notebook to finished product.

Some friends of mine and I have agreed that writers are probably crazy to do what we do. While some drool on the padded wall, unable to tell reality from fiction, and others try desperately to ignore that voice gnawing at the back of their mind, we embrace the darkness and write about it.

Some authors say that they write about things they wish they could do, or write to escape. Not so much with me though. I write things I see in nightmares, because I figure they'll scare someone or I just think they would make a good story. I'm amazed sometimes at the things I see in dreams and how far removed from things in my real life they are. Sometimes the dreams are more entertaining for me than reading or watching movies. Writing them is a way of reliving it for me, much like re-watching your favorite TV shows.

I'll leave you with that. Hopefully you'll enjoy reading these stories as much as I've enjoyed writing them.

THE INVASION

BY JOSEPH SWEET

I

8:45 P. M.

Fran and Bill sat on the back porch of his summer home in Sackets Harbor, New York; Fran on Bill's lap, just holding each other and listened to the sounds of nature all around them.

'This is how it should be,' he thought as he looked across the large span of property, past the cliffs, over the lake; the woods surrounding on all other sides.

Peaceful. Just the two of them.

Then as though on cue, a low sickly moan startled him and he recalled that Jack had passed out earlier in the living room.

'I'd have done better not to remember he was here,' he thought and squeezed Fran playfully to take his mind off the subject.

She stirred and got up.

"Be right back, hon."

Bill sighed, the moment over. The cold of the night air immediately replaced the warmth of her body, and he suppressed the frantic urge to grab her and hold her close out of fear that something would happen in the short time she was gone.

He'd suffered from that paranoia since the first day they met. Perhaps, he would ponder in the times to come, it was a premonition of what would soon befall them.

Jack staggered to the door and mumbled, "How long was I out?"

'Not long enough,' he thought, but replied, "An hour or so." It was times like these when Bill wondered exactly what would become of him. He'd inherited this house from an uncle he hadn't even known, had no job, but didn't really need one with the money which had come with the place. Nearly every relative had asked him at least once or twice what he planned to do with his life, and at the age of twenty three he didn't have a damn clue.

Looking back, it would seem that he had been waiting for something. Throughout his life, there had always been an overwhelming sense that he was destined to do something, yet he was never motivated long to do anything. The frustration came when he stopped to realize that he'd really done nothing of importance his entire life.

'Of course,' he'd always remind himself, *'I am only 23. Got a long ways to go.'* But as each year passed, and that number grew, it began to seem as though his chance to realize his destiny was dwindling before his eyes ...

Jack broke his train of thought with a half formed sentence.

"Must've drank more'n I thought." He was pointing toward the sky. "Tell me you see that too." This second sentence was more structured, as though something had sobered him up a bit.

"No shit." Bill exclaimed, flying to his feet. "What the hell *is that*?"

Lights danced across the sky in a spectacular display of color, like a laser light show. Except, he realized the light was coming down instead of up.

"Fran!" he yelled, wanting her to see this as well.

She came to the door immediately.

"What ... is," she began, stopping in mid sentence, as her eyes fell upon the lights in the sky.

Then it changed, turned green in color and as though someone were turning up the intensity, everything around them began to smoke and catch fire. The lights had taken on small symbolic shapes and they were burning everything they touched.

The roof of the house caught fire almost instantly but where could they go?

Everything was burning. Even the ground was smoking and turning black. Running out into it was most likely suicide.

Thinking quickly, Bill ran into the house and grabbed a leather trench coat, a blanket from the couch and an old bearskin rug off the floor in front of the fireplace. As he ran back out the door, blinded by fear for the woman he loved who was still in shock, half believing everything she was seeing; He tossed the bearskin to jack and wrapped the trench coat around Fran. "Cover yer heads."

Fran was unresponsive.

"Fran."

Nothing.

"Fran ... Honey?"

She turned to him, tears forming in her eyes.

He could empathize with her fear. Deep down he had a feeling that everything was about to change forever, and the only thing, he would think later, that kept him moving just then, was fear for two people he cared about.

Behind them, Bill could hear the crackling of burning wood and what sounded like a beam crashing inward. The porch roof and outer edges were burning as well, and could not long be trusted to keep them safe.

"Come on," he assured her, "We have to go."

She snapped out of it then and he rushed her out into the storm of lights, all of them covering their heads and trying to keep low. The thin fabric over them caught fire almost immediately.

Luckily the cliffs were only a few yards away and the lights, which seemed to be moving in a slow pulsing wave, had not yet reached that area. Once clear, they discarded the burning garments.

In seconds they had made it to the water.

Fran knew exactly what Billy had planned and was the first one in.

He turned to Jack, who had only been to this house twice. "Are you sober enough to swim?"

When he hadn't answered, Bill began to explain. "There are caves under here but you have to swim for a few feet. Nothing big, but I think it's the only way we'll get through this."

Jack nodded and Bill realized then, partially with shock, that he wouldn't have felt terribly bad about leaving him there if he hadn't been able to make it. Later maybe, but not just then.

They were in the water a second later and Bill realized with horror that the temperature was rapidly increasing. Then the strange lights began to pummel the beach. "Get in," he yelled at them, and the three dove under.

As they reached the inner cave, pulling themselves from liquid which was just about burning to the touch, Jack began to throw up. The water started boiling a few seconds later.

For nearly an hour they watched it boil, as the temperature in the cave steadily grew to a nearly unbearable heat. And then it just stopped.

Bill reached over immediately to check the temperature, and instantly pulled back when it scalded the tip of his finger.

It was then that he noticed the burn on his right hand, directly in the center of his palm. He had run almost the entire way with the blanket over him and his hand almost completely palm up to shield his face from being burned.

He gritted his teeth against the pain any movement in this hand invoked. There was some design in the burn which couldn't entirely be made out due to the swelling.

II

Bill awoke from a blissfully dreamless sleep to a cramped neck, the foul stench of vomit, and someone whispering in his ear. Soft, pleasant in tone, but the words were not at first recognizable.

"Fran?" he asked, but she did not respond.

He opened his eyes.

Fran and Jack were on the floor of the cavern. Jack's throat slit, and Fran - *his Beautiful Fran* - her chest had been torn open by something.

The whispering again. Illegible words.

This thing sitting a short distance to the left of Fran; its face was smeared in her blood, large razor teeth, long black claws, and Ominous, oval shaped, glossy black eyes. Its skin was almost pink.

It looked at Bill. Its eyes, (*if they could be classified as that,*) locked with his, and for a moment the words were as clear to him as if they were of his own language.

"Good. Such great rewards are yours to claim." Bill attempted to back away, but the cavern walls behind him wouldn't allow it. Had he done this? Was that why he would be rewarded? He cried out then.

He awoke for real this time, to Fran shaking him. "It's alright baby. 'Sokay"

From just behind her came Jack's voice. "Have a bad one Bro?"

Bill immediately took Fran in his arms, and kissed her. She was a little startled, but seemed more than willing. When they were done she tugged at his shirt and said, "The water's cooled down a bit. I think we should try and go up."

III
7:05 A.M.

Assuming that the worst was over, they returned to the surface moments later.

Fran stood where she was when they exited the water, staring out over it.

Jack simply looked, a blank expression on his face, which drifted ever so slowly into what threatened to be an oncoming purging of the fast food he'd eaten the night before.

Bill dropped to his knees in the sand.

Dead fish floated everywhere.

"Jesus." he said, "It looks like everything in the lake died."

"Somethin' lived." Jack replied then, pointing out a short distance.

They all followed his gaze and saw that something big was indeed moving only a few yards off shore.

Then a bird flew by overhead.

They all noticed it, but no one commented, as it was no kind of bird any of them had ever seen.

It was large like a pterodactyl, but sleek and stealthy looking like a manta-ray.

It was of course neither of the two and only bore a slight resemblance to either, but that was the best way to describe it.

It swooped down toward the water and snatched up a dead fish in its eagle-like talons. It never made it more than a few feet from that spot, however.

Tentacles shot from the water and an immense creature lifted its head out to swallow it whole.

"What the ..." Bill started, and then realized that he was the only one still standing so close to the water.

"Come on." Fran yelled to him from the cement steps which had been built into the side of the cliff.

Reaching the top, a sort of surrealistic wave of confused unreality swept over them all and they almost forgot the creatures below, if that was possible.

It was as though they had stepped out of their own world and into another.

The Cabin was gone except for a charred shell, barely rising from the ground more than two or three inches in most places. But all around it and as far as they could see, vines and trees had overgrown everything. Mammoth flowers had sprouted from the ground, some of them bigger than the house had been. And the sky was now a near perfect, crystalline blue.

Jack was the first to speak, although it was clearly evident that the humor he feigned was not heart felt. "Dorothy, I don't think we're in Kansas anymore."

Bill almost laughed, but given the circumstances it wasn't actually that funny.

An enthusiastic Bark came from somewhere to the east and they all turned their attention that way.

All things considered, Bill half expected to see a demon with huge wings and a Dog's head flying their way, barking and prepared to lick them to death as it descended upon the group.

'I'm losing my mind.' he thought, on the verge of hysterical laughter.

Much to his surprise and delight however, an Alaskan Husky bounded toward them, across the field of alien vegetation, vines, and flowers.

Fran walked toward the animal, forgetting, if that was possible, the oddities of the moment, and Bill was suddenly grateful for the dog. *'Just hope it's friendly.'* he thought.

"Well *hello*," she said, as though talking to a small child, "Where were *you* hiding out little fella?"

The dog ran up and practically trampled Fran, covering her face in fevered licks, obviously just as happy to see her as she was to see him.

"Watch it there *mutt*," said Bill affectionately to the dog, "That's *my* woman."

The dog looked up, averting his eyes from Bill then back at Fran, lowering his head, and whined a little, then trotted over to Bill and sat looking up as though asking for forgiveness.

"Aww shit," Bill said kneeling down to pet him, "I was only joking buddy."

The dog licked Bill's face once, then looked up at Jack, who'd stood silent the whole time, apprehensive; perhaps hoping that this one would accept him as the others had.

"Don't look at me." he said, "Where were you when we had to go *swimming* and sleep in a *cave*? *You* aren't dripping wet."

They all laughed.

The dog gave a short whine, then barked once at Jack.

This only caused them to laugh even harder.

A bond formed between the four of them in that small space of time, for the dog had done something that nothing else could have. He'd taken away the confusion and the nightmarish quality of the moment and allowed them to forget, at least partially, what they had just been through.

TWO HOURS LATER

Having Gathered what little hadn't burned of their home, Fran and Billy cuddled under an enormous leaf, feeling much like the children had in that Disney movie.

Except that they didn't have a clue as to the origin of their problems.

There was no father with a shrink ray here who would rescue them in the end. Or some Hollywood executive to write them a nice neat exit. Here they would most likely have to make their own happy ending.

"What happened here?" Fran asked, breaking the silence with a question they had all been wanting to ask, but knew none had the answer to.

"I dunno," breathed Billy.

It was all so amazing actually, and Terrifying at the same time. Under the mammoth trees and immense plant life they felt as children lost in a fairy tale world. Knowing now, unlike the boys and girls who read and fantasized about those stories, how frightening it would actually be, yet enthralled by the alien landscape which surrounded.

How this all could have come into existence in the short few hours they waited in the cave was beyond their perception. In such a short time span all they knew had been destroyed and all of this created.

Even the largest trees in the deepest untouched regions of rain forest could not have equaled even a quarter of the size of these.

Jack sat by himself, just a short distance away with their newfound friend.

His quiet worried them both, but what could be said under these circumstances?

IV

APRIL 5TH 2:25 P.M.

We searched what was left of the cabin and found the basement to be pretty much intact.

Some canned food and dried goods which we were able to salvage will last us a few days.

This journals amazing appearance seemed an omen to me. In the ashes among other burned books and items, it had lain. Although I must admit never having seen it before, there were probably lots of things I hadn't yet seen there.

Nothing really had been changed since my Uncle died.

I felt that since I never knew him, the best I could do to keep him alive in me or perhaps give me more and more insight into him, would be to keep his place as it had been when he died.

Maybe he knew I would do this.

I haven't told Fran or Jack that I started this, as the implications of it would no doubt depress them, and we need all the strength we can find.

I of course, as do we all, know the very real possibility that none of us may make it through this alive. Not a one of us has any architectural schooling. So building is, at this early point, beyond us. And since there don't appear to be any houses intact so far, we may be (if you'll excuse the word) fucked.

I must say however, that there is a kind of freedom in it. Wandering along as though in wonderland. Maybe even given the chance to start over again as a race.

That is of course until we meet whatever caused all of this to happen. This is something we don't discuss, and I get chills writing about, but the simple fact must be faced that something caused it.

If anyone should find this journal, I thank whatever Gods still exist, because that means there are more of us out there. But it also means, and I shudder to even think this, that we are dead.

Fran. If I go and you read this, please be strong. I love you. And across whatever distances separate us in death, I will love you still.

She's asleep beside me now with her arm around my waist as I sit with my back against this big ass tree. Jack, and Sanford, we decided to name our canine friend, are sleeping nearby.

I'm getting more and more tired by the second, but I fear sleep. I love Fran with all of my heart, but last night when we were in the cave, I dreamt that I had killed her and Jack.

Jack I wouldn't so much have minded ridding myself of on several occasions.

(Just kidding bro), but Fran?

V

Running. Frantically.

Without direction, just running.

But where was there to go? In the darkness mammoth pillars loomed over him like Demons taunting a small child as he tried to sleep.

Couldn't see. Wouldn't see what he had done.

"Fran ... Oh God, Fran!!!" he cried out. His voice echoing back to him mockingly from the Nightmare forest.

He stopped.

The sweat on his naked body caused the warm night air to seem more like a calm winter wind.

Bill shivered, goose bumps breaking out over his entire body.

He tried to speak but couldn't. A vision was fighting to surface, and he struggled to keep it away as best he could. It came nevertheless.

He stood, a campfire blazing madly, painting everything in demonic flickering light which danced like a thousand ghoulish pixies across the surface of whatever it illuminated.

And then it gave light to what he did not want to see.

Jack, his body charred and burning slowly, the life long choked out of him.

And the other.

He wanted to turn away, but this was a memory not a dream, and then he had looked. He was powerless to stop this change of direction in his gaze.

Fran. His dear, sweet Fran. Her eyes having been clawed from her head, her throat ripped away from the front leaving almost nothing to keep it attached to the body except what was left of a partially visible spinal column.

He cried out then in desperation. No words came from the unintelligible mass of sound which poured from him. Rage, panic, self loathing, fear. All at once too much for him to handle, and he began to run again. Realizing only now that it was not only sweat his naked body was slick with.

He screamed again and again, one after another, and then a voice came to him through the insanity.

Her voice.

"Hey, it's okay."

"Oh God Fran, forgive me."

"I forgive you baby, it's alright."

"Oh God," he sobbed.

"Your safe now. It's over."

"No." he cried, outraged, still running. "No. Oh God."

"Baby," the phantom Fran assured him. "It's okay."

But it wasn't over, they would come soon. "They're coming."

He was looking into her eyes then. Having faded without even realizing it from one reality to the other. Her eyes, beautiful green. He remembered asking her back in high school if they were her real color and they had been.

Her red hair seemed aglow in the afternoon sun.

'How?' he thought. And then realized that it had been a dream, and sat up, wanting to slap himself for not realizing that immediately, but also grateful.

"Good morning," she said and smiled, but there was a bit of worry in her eyes.

He sat up and pulled her to him, kissed her on the cheek and then lips. His face turned red in embarrassment at knowing that he'd been calling out in his sleep. They held each other for what seemed a blissful eternity and as he pulled away he said, "I love you."

"I know." She replied. "I love you."

"I'm gonna be sick." Jack added from a short distance away.

VI

"So," Fran started after a near eternity of silence over their meal of canned tomatoes, vacuum sealed granola bars from one of a half dozen old MREs which they'd managed to salvage from the wreckage of the cellar and a little tomato tasting water, which they had all split from the canning jar 80% of their meal had just come from. "Who did you think was coming earlier."

Sanford had inhaled his equal portion, but didn't whine and beg for any of theirs, as if he knew the circumstances, and was aware that begging would be severely rude, not to mention tremendously selfish.

"I don't know." he replied honestly, after thinking for a few moments.

"Why were you apologizing?"

"I thought ... I'd lost you." he stated and a tear rolled down his cheek.

Although this was not entirely a lie, telling her what he had dreamt was simply not an option.

"I'm right here baby. We're all here." Hearing her console him after what he'd dreamed, was not what he needed, and he felt his face grow hot with embarrassment again, but he said nothing.

They held each other for a long while then.

Jack had wandered off, which was probably good since this would have most likely made his stomach turn.

Sanford bolted to his feet, obviously having decided that this affection could be shared, and trotted over to them, licking first Fran, then Bill.

A tiny giggle escaped Fran and she ran her fingers over Sanford's coat.

Bill smiled. Because it was expected. Because the situation did offer enjoyment to Fran. Because he knew he should, but inside he was feeling more and more with each day like a shivering mental patient in the dark corner of a madhouse, in which everyone seemed out to get him. An institution in which all those in charge had been overtaken and killed. Hiding from those he knew to be there in the shadows, reaching with outstretched arms. Feeling for him in the darkness and there was nowhere to run. Soon. Very soon, their probing hands would find him.

VII

APRIL 6TH 11:45 P.M.

Again, they're sleeping.

I don't know what to do. I know now that I will soon have to leave them. My Fran. Leave her. For their own safety. We don't yet have wood enough to waste on a campfire as large as the one in my dream, but when we come across some, I'll know. Especially because it will be a large amount to have produced a fire as big as what I saw.

If I don't leave, something awful will happen to them.

I can't imagine harming Fran. The concept is beyond me. But I also fear that the dream is only a metaphor and that somehow just being near them will put them in danger. I can't describe to you why I feel this way, I just do. And as much as I will suffer, if I can save her life by leaving, so be it.

VIII

"Billy?" a distant and distressed Fran cried out from beside him.

He instantly slammed the small book closed and placed it in his jacket. "I'm right here." he assured her.

"I can't find you."

He lifted her up, and ran his fingers over the left side of her face.

For an instant he was holding her torn, lifeless body and he almost let go before catching the remaining threads of reality and snapping back.

"Fran, honey, I'm right here."

She snapped awake.

"You okay now?" he asked her.

"Yah." her eyes flickered open and closed for a second, as though on the verge of falling back to sleep, then widened again, alert; perhaps having thought better of it, and focused on him.

"I couldn't find you."

"I'm right here," he repeated, wondering if she were having premonitions of his departure.

"Good," she said, and pulled him down on top of her.

Afraid that he wouldn't be in the mood, but surprised nevertheless to find his ever faithful little friend eager to accomplish the task at hand, his mind suddenly fell upon Jack.

"What about him?" he asked, feeling that having sex a few feet from your friend may be a touch insensitive.

"He's sleeping. We'll be quiet."

They made love for hours, and fell asleep in each other's embrace, wrapped in an enormous plant leaf.

He felt a bit like Adam must have felt in the garden of Eden. Except, he thought as he drifted off to sleep, Adam hadn't known what to do with that oddly shaped extra limb, and he did.

Smiling, having forgotten - as incredible as that was - the menacing nightmares, consciousness faded.

This time there were no dreams of murder, just blissful, black nothingness; and the warmth of Fran's body drifting to him from somewhere above it all.

IX

Billy awoke instantly in the darkness.

Fran mumbled incoherently but did not awaken.

'God,' he thought, *'Am I dreaming this time?'*

A short way to the left Jack was snoring away.

Sanford was only inches from him, kicking his feet and whining a little, as though he too were having a nightmare.

Then someone else moved. Somewhere behind him. He stood quickly, facing in that direction, and caught a glimpse of something that wasn't human. It was about six feet tall, pale, almost pink flesh, and a large head, but he hadn't seen its face.

He didn't need to see its face. He'd seen it in the dreams. It would have glassy black eyes, two small barely noticeable nostrils and a large mouth with razor sharp teeth.

Perhaps the dreams had been a metaphor, and he was endangering them just by being there, but now the creatures knew where they were.

A growling sound startled him suddenly. Sanford had awakened, and was growling at what appeared to be just shadows in the opposite direction from the creature he'd just glimpsed.

Fran stood next to him, both of them forgetting that they had nothing on for clothing.

Jack sat up then, looking over at them, his eyes wandering over Fran's near perfect body a little longer than Bill liked. Fran noticed it immediately and began to get dressed, pulling on a pair of sweat pants and a sweat shirt.

She threw Bill a pair of jeans which he'd been wearing earlier, and he slipped them on, always keeping an eye on the woods around them.

Something moved then, this time both Jack and Bill saw it.

Fran followed their gaze, but it was already gone.

Sanford's growling grew even louder, and finally he started barking viciously at the trees, although he seemed to be unsure of the exact direction to which he should be concerned.

One thing was certain, he didn't seem interested in the area behind him.

Bill, thinking quickly, grabbed Fran's arm and said, "Get your bag."

He then grabbed his own pack, and Jack, not having much, was at their side in a couple seconds.

Fran stood a second later, having shoved everything she had into hers.

"When I say go, we all run that way." Bill told them.

"Why *that* way?" Asked Jack.

"The dog's not *barking* that way."

"Good enough for me." replied Fran.

Just as he was getting ready to say it, something came from the shadows.

Fran's eyes widened, and she seemed poised to scream, but nothing came out.

Bill realized instantly that it was her the creature was heading for.

Thinking quickly, he reached down and grabbed a piece of wood which was still burning in the fire and threw it at the monster.

It fell backward with a screech which made all of their skins crawl, and Sanford was on it, biting and clawing.

“Go!” he yelled, and they all ran.

The trees passed them fluidly on all sides, and after each one, he was certain one of those creatures would be waiting, but after running for fifteen minutes or more, it was obvious that they weren’t being followed.

‘They don’t have to,’ he thought. *‘They have me to lead them to us.’*

“Stop.” he yelled, then fell to his knees. Electricity seemed to be coursing through his veins. His arms went out involuntarily, and the feeling built until he thought his head would explode. Darkness drifted quickly over everything and he lost consciousness.

X

Fran ran to him.

“Bill?” She rolled him over from where he’d fallen face down, convulsing. His body fell limp in her arms a few seconds later.

“Jesus,” Cried Jack, “What’s wrong with him?”

Just then Fran realized that it had been slowly growing a little brighter. The trees had been too tall and too wide at the top to let in the light until the sun was over the horizon.

She looked around then, “I don’t think they like sunlight.”

Bill twitched a couple of times in her arms.

“Wake up baby.” she said softly, but he didn’t seem to have even heard her.

XI

Bill awoke on a marble floor.

People were gathering nearby. But as he looked in their general direction, his view was diverted from them to the object of their attention.

An immense statue of the creature from his nightmares.

It stood with its arms out, like a savior, offering forgiveness.

Bill wasn't fooled.

The people were dropping to their knees.

Suddenly his head was filled with sound. A harsh mixture of voices, blending together to form what began to become clearer as words, though they were unintelligible to him.

Slowly they began to make sense.

"Why do you resist?" the voices had calmed now in tone. Soft, soothing.

He wanted to say, *'Because you're evil.'* but quickly found that he couldn't speak.

"There is no other way but death."

Flashes of Fran dead began to stream though his mind then, accompanied by that soft voice, and while he fought the images, the voice began to become clearer and clearer.

There was no resisting it.

"We've already won. Only a fool would think he stood a chance. Join us. Rid yourself of the others, before they find out what you're becoming and turn on you."

Then laughter echoed out to him as the flashing images changed to that of a simplistic drawing of an eye, much like the symbol on his hand. Then in a flash, a strain of D. N. A. which appeared to be changing. Then blood cells which also appeared to be changing in shape. Now he saw himself. Then one of them, only it wasn't. It was him. It was what he was becoming. Like them in a lot of ways, but with enough human D. N. A. surviving to retain most of his facial features. His nose had sunken in and the whites of his eyes had gone black, as well as his iris.

"No!" he cried.

Far away, barely audible, he heard Fran saying, "Wake up baby."

He struggled now, knowing that he was only dreaming this, but it would not fade. He was running through the woods again. Something was behind him, but in the darkness he couldn't see it. Horrible mocking laughter.

Suddenly he awoke.

No one was in sight.

He wanted to call out, but was afraid.

He remembered now that he'd collapsed and wondered if he'd caused the others to be taken.

Maybe they'd tried to help him and been attacked.

Then there was growling.

As he looked up, he saw Sanford inching in his direction, poised to attack.

"Do it boy." he said, tears welling in his eyes, "Kill me."

"Bill! What's wrong with you?" Fran scolded from a few feet to the left.

"Fran!?" he cried excitedly, jumping to his feet, his suicidal urges forgotten for the moment. But Sanford had not forgotten.

The dog leapt on him, biting into his left arm.

Bill struggled as the animal threw its body back and forth, causing its teeth to burrow deeper into his flesh.

With a thunderous bang, Sanford fell to the side.

"Wha ..." he started, then saw Jack standing there, no more than ten feet away with a shotgun.

The dog twitched beside him, but was dead.

Fran ran to him, lifting his arm, her fear for him turning instantly into shock as she did so. It was as he saw this change in her that he realized his arm didn't hurt.

Looking down he saw that in spite of all the blood, his arm was whole.

There was however, as he quickly found, several scars in the spot that had been bitten which looked to be a few years old.

"What's happening?" Fran asked, her voice wavering slightly with fear.

"I think I know." he said.

XII

Fran and Jack sat disbelieving when he finished telling them about the dream he'd had after passing out. He left out the part, of course, about the voice telling him to kill them.

"There *has* to be a sane explanation bro," began Jack, "You *aren't* becoming an *alien*."

"Yah babe," said Fran, inching closer to him, placing an arm around him, "It's just a bad dream. We'll figure it out."

"Maybe you're right." he said, more for them than for actually believing it himself. It was what they needed to hear. But deep down he wanted to tell them about the other dreams. To prepare them for what might happen. A desperate and perhaps more selfish part of him wanted Fran, however, didn't want to leave her. That side of him knew he'd go insane without her. So he waited, closing his eyes and pulling Fran tight to him. A small part of him hoped they'd find a solution.

"We'll figure it out." he repeated.

After a few moments of silence, a thought came to Bill. "Where'd you guys find the gun?"

Jack looked up, startled out of deep thought. Then excitement lit his face and he jumped to his feet. "There's a couple more too."

"Where?" Bill asked.

"We found a truck." came Fran's reply.

"Sorry bro ..." started Jack, "With all the excitement I guess we both forgot."

XIII

While Bill had slept, once all attempts to awaken him had failed, Fran and Jack had paced back and forth for close to an hour.

Then Jack had noticed what looked like the back bumper of a truck, just barely visible behind a tree which had fallen over the mouth of a cave.

Had the light not reflected off the bumper, they'd never have even noticed the opening.

After a few minutes Jack had crawled inside. There'd been room to walk around once he got down in it.

Five minutes later he'd emerged from the mouth of the cave with a shotgun.

"There's enough ammo in there to start a small war."

"What about a driver?" Fran had asked.

"Must have just had it parked in the cave incase of rain. Probably had a hunting camp set up."

There was no sign of a camp but then again, there'd been almost no sign of their house when they'd returned from the cave.

The dog had started barking then, and Fran had come just in time to hear Bill tell it to kill him.

XIV

"Well let's go get whatever we can from it." Bill said with a smile.

They all went then, seeming happy to have something that would take their minds off recent events.

The truck was a pretty beat up, maroon colored, Ford F-150. It looked as though the outside of it had been burned pretty badly.

"This truck wasn't stored in here by a hunting party." stated Bill.

"What do you mean?" asked Fran.

Jack simply waited for an answer as well.

"It's burned, and some of these markings match the symbol burned into my hand. He came here to hide."

"So where is he?" questioned Jack.

"I would say that little alien hunting party got him, most likely."

Bill noticed something then, and moved past them to the truck, reaching inside, and pulled a pair of sunglasses from the visor.

When he put them on, he noticed that Fran and Jack were staring at him.

"What? The sun is *really bright*." As the words poured from his mouth, he realized something they'd overlooked. The aliens hadn't had much time to run since the sun came up.

"What's wrong?" Fran asked, seeing the look on his face.

He reached inside then, and fumbled around for a few seconds.

The headlights came on.

A high pitched, inhuman screeching sound filled the cave as maybe a half dozen aliens shielded themselves from the light, and cowered further into the darkness out of sight.

Only a few feet away was the body they'd been feeding on. Most likely the prior owner of this truck.

"Jesus!" Jack blurted.

Fran let out a short startled scream, but otherwise said nothing.

"Let's try and get this thing out of here before nightfall." Bill said with a tinge of fear evident in his voice.

"I'll bet they didn't even know he was here until they came to this cave for shelter from the sun."

XV

Three hours later, Jack, Bill and Fran had the log moved from the mouth of the cave.

They'd turned off the headlights to conserve the battery, but a large flashlight had been found among some food and other things in the back of the truck.

Using it to light their way, they ventured slowly into the cave toward the front of the truck.

Jack got in on the passenger side, obviously not wanting the responsibility of driving. Fran sat in the middle and Bill slowly eased into the Driver seat.

Nothing could be seen of the aliens in the darkness ahead.

Bill turned on the headlights then.

At least six of them were standing before the vehicle, covering their eyes.

Then slowly they uncovered them and ran for the truck, as they realized that the artificial light couldn't hurt them.

Bill turned the key and the engine roared into life, locking his door with the other hand.

One was on the hood now, its huge razor teeth barred, black, oval shaped eyes seeming to be locked on the driver.

He backed out into the daylight and it shrieked in pain, falling from the hood.

Its flesh was smoking and blistering.

Slowly Bill remembered this cave. It'd been here for years, though the terrain around it had changed extensively. A road had been nearby. Surely all of it hadn't been destroyed. He drove for it then, and in minutes, burst through the bushes onto asphalt.

The road was hardly damaged. Here and there a gigantic root had made its way under and forced a section of pavement up, but other than that it was as it had been.

"Sackets is that way I think." Jack cried out excitedly, pointing over Fran and Bill, then realized they probably knew that.

"Do you really think it would still be there?" asked Fran.

"Only one way to find out." replied Bill, and turned in that direction.

XVI

Bill came to a sudden halt.

"What are we stopping for?" asked Fran.

"Look." he replied.

Fran and Jack saw it instantly. There was a large metal gate at what looked to be the entrance to the town of Sackets Harbor. Although there'd been no intact buildings so far, the town appeared to be in great shape.

"It's still there!" Jack cried out in excitement.

"Yah." Bill said with obvious suspicion in his voice.

"What you thinking babe?" asked Fran.

Bill reached behind the seat into the extended cab where a small storage area was and pulled out a pair of binoculars he'd noticed earlier.

Once he'd looked for a few moments, he put the truck in reverse and backed away. A few seconds later he found a good spot and pulled into the woods.

"What are you doing?" asked Jack, disappointed at the thought of not going into town.

"I don't want him to see us," Bill stated.

"Who, baby?" Asked Fran, seeming concerned.

"The guard." he replied. "He doesn't seem to have noticed us yet."

"There's a guard?" questioned Fran, "That's weird."

"Well, maybe when the shit hit the fan the military got involved. There's always been at least a little military action in town. I don't think it's anything to worry about." Jack stated.

"Even so, I'd rather we came up on the place from the woods, so we can watch for a bit before we go in."

"What you got planned bro?" Jack asked now.

"I don't know," he stated. But that was a lie. He had an idea, or at least a slight bit of foreknowledge as to what he was planning. He knew he needed to get away from them for their own good. Perhaps this was the best way. If the people beyond the gate were hostile, and he went in alone, if he didn't make it out, Fran and Jack would know and get away. And he would kill two birds with one stone.

Fifteen minutes later they'd come within a few yards of the gate.

After a few moments had passed in silence, Bill knew for certain what his plan was. Removing his makeshift Pack, and handing it to Fran, he said, "I'm going in."

When she started to argue, he cut her off with, "If it's safe, I'll come back for you guys."

"Bro." Jack started disapprovingly, but silenced when he saw the look on Bill's face.

"If I don't come back, you two get as far from here as you can."

"*I* should go," Jack said.

"I'm going."

"Baby, *why*? Wouldn't we be safer *together*?" Fran argued.

"You both have to trust me on this." He kissed Fran and hugged her for a few moments.

With that he walked away, fighting not to look back out of fear that the tears he was resisting would spring forth.

The guard didn't even flinch at first, until he came within a foot of the gate. Then as though awakening from a trance, he snapped fully alert and aimed his rifle at Bill's head.

"Halt!" he ordered, to which Bill nearly laughed.

Having no military experience, he'd never heard that word used anyplace other than TV, or in movies, and it sounded somewhat ridiculous in reality. But then, he did have a gun to his head.

He threw his hands up, palms forward, certain that this was it.

The guard's eyes widened, his aim faltered, and he lowered his weapon.

The gate opened. Again, this structure, almost overnight. It had been built in such a short period of time and looked old, as though it had been here for years. The metal was slightly rusted. The cement at the bottom, around the outside of it, was cracked and weather beaten.

"Stop!" the guard ordered, to which he came to an abrupt halt once more.

When the guard approached him, his rifle was at his side, as though he no longer feared violence from Bill. He produced a small device that looked much like something a store clerk might use to scan a bar code, except that it was much more advanced. "Give me your hand."

Bill did as he was told.

Much as it had appeared, it was some sort of scanning device.

The guard ran the thin red line of laser light over the marking on Bill's hand, which responded as though it had a mind of its own. A hologram projected upward, seemingly from the symbol, and he saw with horror that it was the creature from his nightmares.

Somehow throughout all of this he held his composure. His widened eyes closing and reopening before the Guard looked up to see, and returning to a placid, uncaring and perhaps slightly impatient look.

The man simply took two steps back and motioned for him to continue on his way.

Bill walked forward, but not into the town he saw before him. A thick liquid, seemingly living wall of reality nearly stopped him from proceeding, but something within made him keep walking. In moments the world he knew, swirled, rippled and faded into a new one.

It was Egyptian in design. Very close to what he had seen in history books, but changed somehow. Nearby buildings - shaped as pyramids except for flat tops and more the size of houses - rose at least three stories high and appeared to descend into the ground even further.

Not far away, enormous statues much like Egyptian Gods, but vaguely different, guarded the entrance to what appeared to be a castle of some sort, although the architecture here defied all logic. Rounded, curving stone rose and extended outward with nothing beneath it for support to hold sectioned platforms.

For a moment he stood breathless, uncertain of what to do, then began walking toward the castle.

He passed others on the sandstone carved brick streets, but none acknowledged his presence.

*

Neither Jack or Fran spoke at first. Neither of them had words to even question what they had just seen. Bill had walked toward the town and everything after five feet from the gate had rippled as though it were a sideways lake, merely reflecting a living town. Then he vanished and the ripple died, smoothed out again.

*

As he approached the entrance, two mammoth doors opened by themselves, and a vehicle which hovered a few feet from the ground shot out and flew past him.

Taking probably the only chance he would get for a while, he dove between the open doors before they could close again.

Once inside, A huge hallway with high vaulted ceilings extended about fifty yards to a hangar, where more vehicles such as the one he had just seen were parked.

Two enormous staircases spiraled upward into shadows to the left and right.

None of this was what made his heart seem to freeze in his chest. In the center of it all, what he at first mistook to be real, a gigantic statue towered over him. The statue from his dream.

A chill moved through him.

Water surrounded the statue on all sides and several people had gathered around it on their knees. This enormous stone version of the creature that plagued his nightmares, seemed to be beckoning to him with its outstretched arms, and he knew in that moment that it had not entirely been his choice to come here. He had been led, and the voices which called to him now - although their language was unknown to him - were completely understood suddenly.

He was to lead them to the survivors so they could be brought here and converted or killed. The thought at once made sense, yet was horrifying. On one hand he knew that it had to be done and the other, was disgusted with himself for having such a thought.

Before Bill knew it he found himself kneeling in front of the statue. As powerful as the urge was to fight those voices, stronger was the need to Listen to what they were saying.

XVII

Fran sat with her back against a tree. Jack was only a few feet away.

"We have to go get him you know." Fran said.

"What about the guard?"

"He let *Bill* through."

"Yah but he was looking at the burn on Bill's hand. Maybe he thought it was a mark of some kind. Ya know ... Like a pass?"

Jack laid on the ground, looking thoughtfully up at the seemingly never ending trunks of trees which surrounded them to the thick ceiling of branches and leaves at the top.

He took a deep breath and said, "Let's give him an hour. If he doesn't come out by then, we'll go in after him."

Uneasy with the thought of waiting at all, Fran replied, "Half an hour."

"Half it is."

XVIII

An entire lifetime of alien teachings were transferred into Bill as he knelt before his teacher.

Languages of different races, anatomies of creatures the human mind had never dreamt of on its darkest day, flight instructions and manuals. New moral values and understandings, which immediately conflicted with what he already knew and believed, but just as he started to fight it, they strengthened and he was powerless to stop them. The human race was a plague, poison to all it touched. And how could he deny it was true? It had mistreated and poisoned its mother planet until she was so sick as to poison her own children.

These new colonies had restored the world to its highest potential. They offered clean energies, and non polluting sources of transportation and production. The survivors of the human race would be allowed to live on as they wished, in a better world. They however, would not tolerate resistance.

Resistance meant a possible defeat of new ways and return to old. The destruction of their newly adopted mother.

All who opposed her would perish.

An image of Fran came to him then. What if she resisted? And she would. He would be forced to kill her.

This was unacceptable.

"No." he cried out.

The link was broken. The voices had stopped. The room spun for a second, and he suddenly felt as though he was going to be sick. It was something akin to withdrawal. As though he had needed those voices in his head, and an essential part of his body had been swiftly and violently removed.

He struggled then to decide what was more important and was embarrassed to realize that he'd even had to ask himself. Of course Humans were more important. His own race. Who may have been destructive and capable of tremendous evils, but were also capable of such awesome good.

Bill noticed a change in the others kneeling then. Their attention had been averted to him. Five of them stood, their eyes glassy but filled suddenly with purpose.

Violence would ensue, it was inevitable. The voices had attempted to teach him their ways and make him submit to their beliefs, but they hadn't expected him to be smart. And he had resisted.

Resistance will not be tolerated.

He realized then that he knew this building perfectly, inside and out.

Turning from the small group, he ran. Toward the hangar. Toward where he knew to be transport vehicles. Translated to English their names roughly would be, S-12, Freight 2-16, the psi-port G-9, and a 230-M. The Psi-Port was the one he needed. It could hold five people and transport to marked locations faster than light travels. Attaining that speed instantly and stopping just as fast, feeling as though it had never moved.

He could hear them just behind, running after him. He knew what they would do and understood why. If they had bought into everything they'd been fed, he was a traitor. A threat to the mother. And he was to be immediately destroyed.

They of course would not take into consideration that this new race had killed most of the human population, invaded our world and taken us hostage.

We would never be free in their world, if they could control our thoughts by making us believe what they wanted us to.

He was in the hangar now, searching for something he had never physically seen but had memories of nevertheless. And then he saw it and perhaps by will to board the ship, its hatch opened for him.

Bill ran up the small ramp which immediately closed behind him and the ship began to rise into the air before he even reached the cockpit.

Slightly amazed, he sat down in the seats provided and waited for it to clear the building.

This hangar had been built completely open at the top, which was nearly four stories high.

Once above the building, he willed its destination to be just outside of the gates, near where his friends would be waiting.

In the blink of an eye the surroundings and elevation changed to just outside the gate. Gunfire erupted from behind, no doubt from the guard.

The side hatch opened as if by his will. Giving the ship a mental command it cloaked, becoming completely invisible to the naked eye. He walked to the perimeter of the cloaking field and signaled for Fran and Jack to enter.

*

"That's it," Fran stated impatiently, "I'm going in there."

Before Jack could stop her she was to the road.

In a flash a hovering vehicle seemed to materialize, and a powerful gust of wind almost knocked her off her feet.

Glaring at it as though it were a creation of her imagination which would no doubt vanish as suddenly as it had appeared, she tried to establish the reality of the situation. It seemed real in every way. Was it possible that it had simply moved much too quickly for her to see?

Gunfire pierced the near perfect silence of the day just then.

It seemed obvious at first that the guard was aiming for the ship. It was then that the vehicle vanished from view.

Fran stared in awe at the spot where it had been hovering seconds ago, refusing to believe her eyes.

The gunfire continued. Looking up, Fran could see that the guard was now firing almost directly at her, but he was either firing blanks or the bullets were vanishing before they reached her.

Just then the fabric of reality seemed to ripple as though it were merely a reflection of what she was seeing in a calm pool, and a rock had been thrown into it.

Bill emerged from the ripple and everything calmed out again.

"Come on." he said, extending his hand.

Her attention switched to Jack who seemed to still be in the same position he'd been in the last she'd seen him, looking as though this new turn of events had left him mentally actionless. He stood up then, deciding that no harm could come to him from Bill. As they approached, Bill vanished back into that same ripple and they followed.

Within seconds they were on the platform leading into the ship they had just seen.

*

Bill had gone straight to the cockpit, but turned to them a second later and said, "Let's go."

"But what about the guard?" asked Jack.

Bill only gave him a troubled look as though he didn't understand what he was concerned about and walked toward the opening hatch.

They followed him to find that they were in the middle of a large field, yet the small ship hadn't even seemed to have moved.

"Where are we?" asked Fran.

"Just outside of what used to be Watertown, New York. Look over there." They followed the direction of his gaze. "The mall used to be right there. You can still see some of it."

"Shit!" Jack replied.

"Either of you didn't happen to find a knife in that truck did you?"

"No," replied Jack, "but you should know I usually have one on me."

He reached under his shirt to his belt then and pulled the small knife from its leather holder, handing it to Bill.

Bill immediately opened it and began cutting into his hand where the symbol was, before anyone could object.

They both watched in horror, then awe, as first he cut the symbol off his hand, then the wound healed into scar tissue.

Bill picked up the piece of flesh and poked around in it with the knife, finally finding what he was looking for. A very small metal cube.

"This is what allowed them to know where I was. There were a few more, but I got them out of me."

"What is it?" asked Fran. Jack remained silent, waiting for the answer as well.

"It's a translocation device," Bill started to explain, "It and billions of others were shot to the surface of the planet. Thousands, maybe more objects, trees, plant life, and even creatures were stored electronically, then duplicated. These recreate them, but there needs to be a grid.

"You mean like teleportation?" Jack asked.

"Exactly, only a little bit better. For every five of these, in the ground, a tree or plant is transported. They intended to destroy the surface of this planet and recreate it as their own was before it was destroyed. They figured we were killing this place anyway, and rather than watch a potential home vanish before their eyes, they moved in and took it over." He paused for a second. "There's also another problem."

"What could shock us after all that?" asked Fran, and he supposed she might be right.

"They excrete genetic material, so that any living thing which survived would become like them. They have a natural telepathic link to each other on a genetic level. While each of them have their own consciousness, they communicate by thought, which would nearly force a recipient of the D. N. A. to succumb to their way of thinking."

"You mean you *are* changing into one of them?" asked Jack.

"No." stated Bill, "Now that they're out of me, I won't change any further than I already have. And the only things which have changed this early, involve strength and regenerative capabilities. The body has to become strong enough to receive the D. N. A. or it will reject it."

"How do you know all of this?" Asked Fran, taking his hand.

He told them then of the statue trying to brainwash him, filling him with knowledge.

"But," he started, "It was *you* that helped me get out of it. I thought of you and the connection was broken. My love for you, and fear of losing you, helped me break free."

"I love you." she sighed, pulling him close to her.

"So what do we do now?" asked Jack.

"I know nearly everything about them. The bastards are like vampires, except they don't feed on blood. We have the advantage during the day, we just have to watch our asses at night."

"Do you really think we can beat them?" asked Fran, pulling away.

"We have to try." he answered.

They all stood then, looking out over the hills, and the sun which was dropping ever closer to the horizon. Perhaps the last humans who hadn't been brainwashed or murdered.

"At least," started Bill, breaking the silence, "They shouldn't know where we are tonight. If we cloak the shuttle we should be safe for now, but they'll find us eventually, and we'll have to be ready to fight.

XIX
DECEMBER 10TH
11:45 P.M.

I hope the story I've left on the previous pages has given you some inspiration. I heard of another small army to the north of here, and we're headed in that direction.

Tune you're radio, if you have one, to 101.2 a.m. If you don't have one, check in the upstairs bathroom, in the closet, by the door. We left one there for you, along with materials and plans to build another one to leave in its place.

The radio station is run by a group which is in direct contact with the army, and now with us. With any luck, they'll still be there.

My wife Fran is eight months pregnant, and we're going to stay here for the duration of the pregnancy and the winter.

When we go, we plan to leave some dried foods and canned goods in the basement. Partially because we can't carry it all, but mainly because I have the feeling we won't be the last ones to inhabit this house.

I wish you luck and I thank whatever gods there are, for they have definitely kept an eye out for us when we needed it. And if you're reading this, there are more of us out there.

I'm sorry it's been so long since I left a journal entry, but we ran across a woman in the ruins of a nearby town.

She'd attempted suicide moments before we arrived. All our time has been spent keeping my wife comfortable and warm and tending to this new woman.

Her name is Veronica, and she seems to be getting better everyday.

I also think Jack is falling for her, and she seems to be warming up to him. You probably don't care, but I hope things go well with them. He's needed a companion so badly all this time, and it finally looks like he may have found someone.

Oh he's had us, sure. But while our friendship has been good for him, he seemed to grow lonelier all the time. Now he appears happy.

I'll leave you now. I'll put this journal on the living room table when summer comes and we leave this place.

We'll be heading North as I said, and we hope to have more people joining us in the future. If you do head that way, be sure to leave this where you found it, perhaps adding your own entries to its pages for those who would come after you.

Best wishes, and good luck.

Yours

Bill Edwards

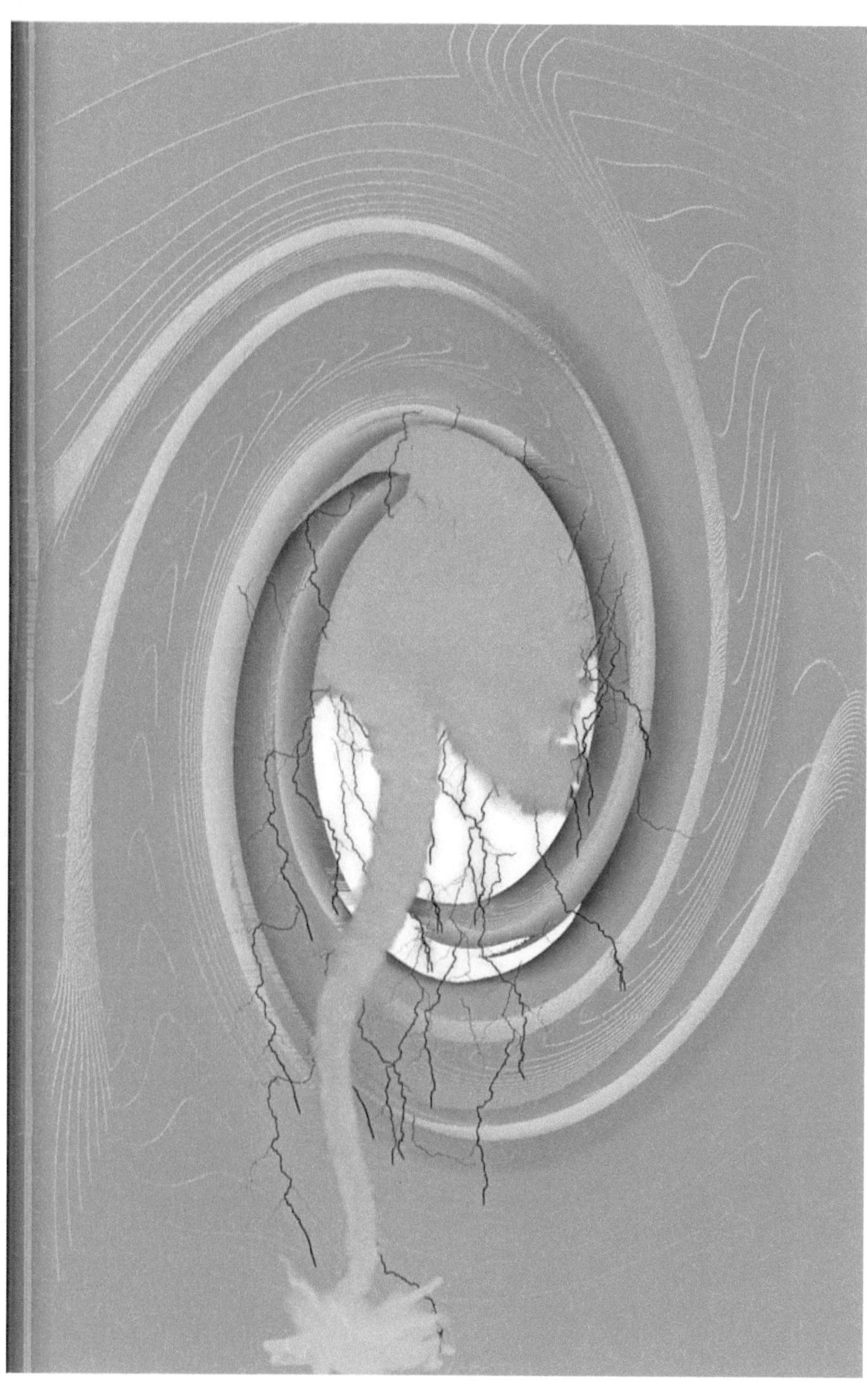

A STORM OF LIGHT

BY JOSEPH SWEET

0

"Ooh, Daddy, that's what I want, can I get that?"

Kate was actually, and perhaps unknowingly jumping up and down a little. It was good to see her in such high spirits. And Phil knew beyond the shadow of a doubt that if she wanted this toy so much, she would have it.

"Can't have it today sweetie, but if you're good, just maybe for Christmas."

Kate grinned, knowing full well, as he did, that meant yes.

At Eleven years old, Kate already seemed to be aware that toys were not merely acquired by parents when they knew their child wanted them. And unlike others her age, if she was denied that which she wanted she would not cry and throw temper tantrums, for she also knew that her father was not as financially well off as he pretended.

Phil was still able to get her most of what she wanted however.

He sighed as they walked through the entrance to KB toys, knowing that he'd be buying something today, but it was worth it, if Kate was happy.

After her mother's death, only two short years ago, she had gone through periods of depression, in which she wouldn't talk. Now that she seemed so alive and full of energy, he would not allow her to be disappointed. Not now when they were a family again.

The lights flickered.

For an instant Phil thought he saw a long deserted, cob web infested store, but it was gone so quickly that it couldn't have been more than his imagination.

Still, he had seen so much detail in that split-second vision.

There a doll on the shelf had fallen to the floor, covered in at least a year's dust. There a shelve had fallen inward, spilling its contents all over the aisle.

A sudden wave of paranoia swept over him and he was tempted to pick Kate up and flee this place, in front of everyone, in spite of what they would think. Just run.

But the moment passed and he did nothing.

Obviously overcome by the onslaught of brain-washing signs and packaging, Kate walked through the isles, zombified, and while she did so Phil became alerted to something she had not noticed, or forgotten to look for. Something she had been begging him for ever since a commercial had prematurely advertised it over a month ago.

Playing the secret agent of the almighty Santa, a deity of miraculous gift giving to children worldwide, (*which Kate herself had been deprived of at an early age by some little snot on the school bus, who's parents had never allowed him to believe in the myth himself,*) he crept toward the counter reaching for his wallet.

The woman, no older than twenty - perhaps actually nineteen or even eighteen - gave him a warm smile which was just a slight bit seductive. Phil doubted if she was aware of this. And even if she were, he was at the least ten or eleven years older.

For a moment he was tempted to flirt back, but was struck with the most terrible feeling that there was something infinitely wrong with her, and suddenly her attractiveness melted away for him. Phil himself had never been a presumptuous person, always giving people the benefit of the doubt; assuming the worst, only when it became futile to think otherwise. But here and now, on this day, it was as if everything had changed. As though the reality he had known throughout his life had become his enemy and he was just beginning to realize it.

He did not wish to converse with the woman, but saw no other choice in the matter, for he didn't want to offend her. She was after all very attractive, but he just wasn't feeling well.

"How are you doing today sir?" When he didn't answer her question right away she continued, "Is there anything I can help you with?"

Her smile widened as though she herself was as intrigued by the infinite number of possible answers to that question as he was. This, he thought, was probably his imagination as well. Either that or she was trying not to laugh at his odd behavior.

"Time flux." he said, unable to get more than the game title out.

For a second she seemed at a loss, then an expression of realization passed over her and she said, "The game?"

He nodded.

"PlayPod or Dreamscape?" meaning game systems, but for a moment he was lost.

Phil's face turned bright red, as he realized what she meant, feeling like the idiot of all time and replied, "PlayPod."

The girl turned, taking a box down from the display rack behind her.

"Oh, do you have paper? I'm with my daughter and I don't want her to see it through the bag."

He nervously glanced back at Kate who was just visible now at the end of an aisle of toys and the girl followed his gaze.

"Tell ya what. All we have is plastic up here, but I have one in the back room with my stuff. Can you wait just a second?"

"Sure." He could feel his face growing hot again. How he could have thought anything bad about this woman was beyond him now. "That'd be ... Great."

She smiled. Veronica her name was, he realized now by the name tag, although as he looked at it he was aware that she probably thought he was looking at something else.

She disappeared to the back of the store an instant later and returned almost as quickly with a large paper bag, which she'd no doubt purchased something in earlier that day before work.

As Veronica handed it to him, her gaze switched to a short ways behind him. "Oops, here she comes."

With that she plucked the bag back from his hands, dropped the game inside, folded it around the package like wrapping paper and taped it shut with a paid sticker.

"That'll be Fifty three forty nine." she paused. "Wait." Typed some more at the cash register. "Forty eight, fifteen."

"What'd you do?"

"I gave you a store workers discount."

"Wow," he said. About to say *'you didn't have to do that,'* but she knew this, and settled for just, "Thanks."

"You're welcome." She smiled.

"What's that?" Kate inquired as she approached the counter.

Then she forgot the paper bag, as her eyes fell upon the promo poster for Time Flux. Phil couldn't help but wonder how she had missed it on the way in.

She drew in a deep breath, her eyes widening. "They got it!" She looked from him to the lady at the counter, to the game hanging on the wall. Daddy, that's the game I was telling you about. It's *soooooo awesome*."

"Actually," Veronica interrupted. "Your Daddy was just asking me about it, but someone called in about five minutes before you got here and put the last one on layaway." She winked at Phil. "We *do* have some more coming in *next* week."

Phil tried to keep from grinning, "How's that? We'll come in next week and look, Okay?"

"Okay," she agreed excitedly.

As they walked away, veronica said, "Looks like you've got a winner there,"

He did smile then, raising the bag and waving. "Thanks."

"Guess what?" he asked Kate, as they neared the mall exit.

"What?"

"I got you something."

"What is it? Can I have it now?"

They were almost at the doors.

"I don't know." he replied, teasingly.

"Please?" she begged in a long drawn out voice, although she knew he would give in ...

They were at the doors now.

"Okay fine," he said, and handed her the gift, which was just distorted enough by the amount of paper surrounding, that it appeared to be much bigger than the game packaging. "But that's one less present for Christmas."

She had filled him in a little on the story line which was science fiction in nature. Involving a couple cops, a teenaged girl and time travel. Apparently some scientific experiment had caused a rip in the fabric of time and they had been caught in the middle of it, trying to stop some monsters out of the future from destroying time itself.

The whole thing was far more complicated than he cared for, but she would no doubt explain it to him as she learned the game ...

That feeling of dread came over him again, but he was too caught up in awaiting Kate's reaction and pushed it away.

"You got it!" she squealed. And he knelt down to receive her hug. Then they were walking out the doors, the moment of bizarre apprehension almost completely forgotten. A smile spreading across his face.

Then it was back full force. The sun was just below the horizon, leaving the sky in shades of dark blue and ominous red clouds. The only problem with this was that when they had arrived only two hours before, it was only Twelve O'clock in the afternoon.

An engine revved. A large engine. Perhaps some trucker preparing to head back for the highway.

Something was wrong though. Horribly wrong.

"Daddy?" an unusually unconfident and scared Kate asked.

There was no denying it now. She had sensed it as well.

Putting his hand on her shoulder, he attempted to assure her that everything was fine; fighting his own superstitious belief that something horrible was about to happen.

The world had changed however, no matter how insane it seemed. He knew it was true.

The engine revved one last time and tires squealed on pavement, as the driver let off the brakes.

A Mack truck was bearing down on them. There was no time to act.

"Daddy?" Kate screamed this time. That one word snapped him out of his paralysis and he pushed her out of the way.

The last thing he saw was a pale, menacing face. A dog-like snarl forming a ghastly grin.

The driver. Death personified.

THUD.

Darkness.

I

Cain reached the edge at roughly Six O'clock in the afternoon.

Retrieving his compass from the inside left pocket of his jacket, he checked the direction one last time.

He'd been dead on as thought. Then it happened again.

The event he'd been tracking.

A narrow beam of light shot into the sky, then fanned out and vanished. Bolts of lightning rippled from the center of ominous black clouds and signs of a storm began to show.

Last night's dream came to him again.

He'd been running. A storm had begun, and a mammoth tornado been spawned.

Just ahead, was a large hill. Certainly no cover there, but perhaps on the other side there would be.

He'd moved on.

As he neared the top, the winds became so strong that he could barely stay standing. The storm was almost upon him.

He fought with every ounce of strength to get to the other side of that hill.

He'd been here before. There was a church.

'Foolish.' he thought in that instant, 'I've never been this close to the rift before.' but he knew otherwise it seemed. 'I've dreamed this,' he thought then.

Soon a large cathedral came into view, seeming very out of place here in the middle of nowhere, but it would do for shelter. He reached it just as the storm threatened to lift him into the air, and after fighting for a few seconds, managed to get the large double doors open.

It was dark inside, except for two candles, far off by the altar, which had been dressed with freshly picked flowers. A woman who had been kneeling before it, rose to greet him.

"Have to get underground," he'd said.

The whole place shook in that instant, and just when he feared the entire building would be ripped from its foundations, he'd awakened.

This dream had haunted him for a year, coming now and then, but lately it was every night. He longed to know who the woman was. She was no one he had ever seen before in his life. Either a complete construction of his mind, or something more.

Just over the next rise, left of the old highway, was a building. A shopping mall. It would do for shelter. A chill ran swiftly up his spine, and he ignored it the best he could. This was real, not a dream.

His mind wandered then to a question of safety. This close to the rifts, mutants were common. He eyed the mall once more, wondering if it was worth the risk.

As the winds picked up, sounds of a revving engine drifted his way. A large engine.

Cain froze in his tracks.

Encountering other life these days, was not usually a good experience.

Kneeling down he removed a leather pack, took out a small pair of binoculars and scanned the distant mall for the source of the sound.

What he saw made his blood run cold.

A Mack truck. With what looked to be "Mall Security" spray painted on the doors. Circling a group of cars, like a vulture around dying prey.

Something moved among the parked cars and trucks.

He quickly moved with it, attempting to catch another glimpse of it, and then it came into view.

A little girl, obviously frightened nearly into hysterics, cowering among the vehicles: Her clothing spoke of another time, still new and clean.

Another chill moved through him.

Cain saw no other choice than to become involved, and he descended the hill side at a run; returning the bag to his back as he went, and placing the binoculars around his neck.

As he reached the parking lot, he realized that he would have to remain unseen until he got close enough, or the whole thing would be ruined.

Dodging among the cars, he came closer and closer to the crying girl, who was moving among them in a daze, screaming for her daddy. She was headed back towards the mall.

Cain realized then that the truck had stopped, engine revving; Just short of the doors, waiting for her to come out in the open.

She was almost there, and Cain saw what she was headed for; Her eyes locked on the target, screaming. "Daddy!!!"

The man on the ground was dead for certain.

Cain broke into a run for the girl, closing the distance quickly.

Tires squealed as the trucks' driver let off his brakes.

He was almost close enough.

"Daddy daddy ..." the little girl screamed.

The truck was bearing down on her.

Cain reached the girl, snatching her up and dodging between two cars, just as the truck passed through the section she had been in.

The girl screamed furiously, wanting to reach her father. Needing to reach him.

Cain ran for the doors.

Once inside, he set her on the floor, where she immediately attempted to scramble to her feet and head for the exit again.

He grabbed hold of her and sat her down.

"No!"

She seemed to understand.

Her gaze then shifted to something behind them. A bag. She'd dropped it when they entered.

"You want that?" he asked.

She nodded.

"Will you stay put if I get it for you?"

Another nod.

"Okay, I'm going to go get it. Stay right here."

Cain peeked into the bag as he picked it up and was baffled by its contents. *'A video game?'* Nevertheless, he returned it to her.

'What the hell is she going to do with it?' he wondered.

There was no electricity, hadn't been for years. Somewhere around forty years to be exact.

She accepted the item, removing it from the bag, staring at it.

"Yah," he said, to himself. "*This* is what I needed. A techno-junky kid in the second dark age, and a psycho-trucker mall-cop."

And then he realized that he was most likely directly in the center of the event he'd been tracking for the last two weeks, and he had to know where she had come from. How her and her father had gotten here. Was there a town nearby?

None of these questions got out however.

The truck smashed though the doors, spraying glass and debris at them.

Cain immediately dove for the girl on instinct.

The truck pulled back out of the building and drove away.

He grabbed her and headed deeper into the unlit mall.

II

Heather left the Chinese restaurant in the food court with lunch for everyone at the office. Todd had offered to go in on it with her, but she'd lost the bet, not him. And she knew that he only offered because he liked her. The two of them were nothing alike and there just was no point in allowing him to think they ever would be.

Two more stops before she headed back. Corbin Books and Ames.

As the food court got further and further behind, she became uneasy. It was as if she were walking into dark woods at night without a flash light or lantern, and not a fully populated mall.

A few feet ahead, the center of this building, a huge fountain's water changed from red to green and back and forth. A rather cheaply constructed decoration considering the size of the place and the money which was made from it.

As she gazed into the waters a feeling of unreality swept over her and the lights flickered.

The sounds around her seemed to halt in that brief instant and then start again.

She stopped abruptly, wondering if she were having a nervous breakdown.

The lights went out again and this time they stayed out. Once more all sounds seemed to die with them.

Heather froze, attempting to push aside the fear building within her.

People should be cursing the power outage, bumping into each other, at least talking and questioning the cause of the darkness.

There was only silence.

"Hello?" she called out, putting her arms before her, where there should be someone, anyone. The place had been packed. No more than a few inches in any direction there had been so many people. There had to be someone else here.

Slowly her eyes began to adjust to the darkness. The ceilings in these immense mall corridors were open at the top with fogged over windows.

Although there weren't many of them, some light was managing to leak through.

There was no-one to be seen.

III

Victor took his time, looking through movie after movie that he knew he wouldn't buy.

The man at the counter had been following him around as though he thought he was going to steal something.

Every time he looked back, the man was there watching with that same look of utter distaste.

'Fuck him.' he thought. If the man wanted to be a prick, then he'd take as long as he could before buying what he came in here to get anyway.

Perhaps it would be better to display his aggravation with being followed and leave the place without spending a dime. That, however would just prove to the man that he *was* in here to do something illegal. So, he'd just wander around aimlessly for a couple hours, then pay for what he wanted and leave. This way he could both waste the pricks time, and prove him wrong in the same instance. His logic probably wouldn't hold up under a good deal of scrutiny, but it worked for him, and that was the important part.

A wave of dizziness fell over him then and he almost lost his footing, reaching out to grab hold of the DVD display rack beside him.

His hand came back matted in at least a years dust, but when he looked back at the racks he found them to be as clean as could be, with nothing having been displaced. Yet surely he had felt a few DVDs fall over as he'd reached out.

And had he blinked, or had the power gone out for a second?

The man was staring at him now, not seeming to be concerned that one of his customers had almost fallen, but shocked, as though he wasn't sure what he'd just seen.

Victor stood there for a moment, and then the power did go out.

Slowly he turned back toward the front of the store, trying not to lose his bearing.

Using the racks as a guide he made his way forward, expecting to bump into someone at any moment. In fact shouldn't he be hearing confused voices? In his experience people in situations like this were panicky, stupid animals.

He half expected to hear someone ask, "Hey, did the power go out?" to which he would be forced to almost say, "No dumb-ass, God decided you were too stupid to waste good eyesight on." Or hear someone speculating about a terrorist attack. Wasn't that just the shit lately. Terrorists this, terrorists that.

Were it not for a strong feeling that something was incredibly wrong, he'd have just stood there waiting to hear someone and move toward them. But he had to prove to himself that this was just an ordinary power outage. That there were people in this place. That he wasn't alone, because it sure as hell felt that way. Suddenly he felt like one of those panicky dumb animals he so loved to make fun of. "Hello?" he called out. "What's ..."

"... going on?"

Heather spun to her left immediately. A voice had broken the silence.

While it still was far from normal in a building which had been crowded only a few seconds before, one would have to do.

"Hey." she called out, "Where are you?"

"Oh jeez." the voice replied, "Thank god. I thought I was by myself here."

'You aren't the only one,' she thought, but replied, "Keep talking, I'm coming your way."

"What happened?"

Things were getting a little easier to see now. Her eyes had adjusted to the low light, and she could see the man emerging from Video Planet.

"I'm not sure." she answered, "I think there was a power outage."

"I was hoping that was all, but where is everyone?"

"I don't know."

IV

Frank listened to the mechanic for about fifteen seconds. Fifteen seconds too long in his opinion. Then decided that he had heard enough. "For *Christ's sake man*," he began, "I'm not a *mechanic*."

"Sorry," the man started although it was obvious that he'd liked to have said, *'listen buddy, fuck off.'*

"I don't need to know what's *wrong* with it. That's why I brought it to *you*. Just *fix* the damn thing. Don't explain to me *why you're doin' it*, or *how*. I don't need to know all that crap. Just figure out what you *have* to do, tell me *how much*, fix it and be *done with it*. You're wasting my time."

"*Whatever* pal. Should be about a half hour."

"Good! See how *easy* that was?" Somewhere deep down where he still housed emotions, Frank knew that he'd probably ask the man what had been wrong with the car and why it cost so much to fix afterwards. And he knew no explanation would be good enough for him, so he felt a little bad. He didn't know why he acted the way he did and most of the time he didn't care to waste time thinking about it. A few seconds passed however, and that thought, which had only been a momentary revelation as to how much of an ass-hole he really was, had been forgotten.

As he turned away from the mechanic, who was probably more than pleased to see him go, a sound came to him.

Frank had been in the army for six years, and one thing he recognized without missing a beat was the sound of a bomb being dropped from the sky.

Without a moments hesitation, he dove for the floor, knowing that this was probably it.

It hit while he was in midair, and for an instant he thought he was dead already.

The building disappeared in bluish arcs of electricity all around him, and he saw many things, in the space of a second. It happened in waves where the building around him faded in and out, seeming to be aged, then new, then in ruins, and at the last he was falling into a huge crater.

A moment later the crater was gone and he fell face first onto cement in darkness.

V

Heather and Victor had just exchanged names and were debating on whether to search out the mall or just leave.

“NOOOOOO!” a little girl screamed from somewhere nearby, “Daddy?!”

The two of them broke into a run, coming around a corner only inches from Cain and the girl who was struggling to get away from him.

The man’s clothing appeared to be hand made, and not very well done.

“Hey!” Victor called out, getting the man’s attention. As he turned, startled, Victor punched him, sending him to the ground.

The girl, free now, made for the doors. As her feet fell on broken glass, Victor’s attention was drawn that way, and his jaw dropped as he took notice of the destroyed entrance.

“What the ...” he began, then realized what the girl was running for. “No wait!” he cried, running after her. He was outside, before he realized the danger.

The girl was only a couple feet from her father when Victor snatched her up, and it was then that he heard the trucks engine bearing down on them.

He knew there wasn't enough room to run to safety, so he went as far as he could before the large vehicle was almost on them, and tried to jump the rest.

As he dove forward with the girl in his arms, the truck hit his right leg, sending him spinning toward the ground. Victor gave a startled cry, and then the air was forced out of his lungs by the impact, as his body hit the pavement.

*

Heather watched in horror, as the truck hit Victor, and began to circle around for another pass.

The blade of a very sharp knife was pressed against her throat suddenly and an arm went 'round her midsection, pulling her back.

"Who are you people?"

"My names Heather." She answered quickly.

"What's in the bags?" he could smell the freshly cooked food, but wouldn't allow himself to believe it.

"Lunch for my co-workers."

"*Liar*!" he hissed.

"No, *really*."

"Where'd you get it?"

"The *food court*." she stated as though this should be obvious.

"Liar."

"I *swear* it's the truth mister."

"There hasn't been food here in nearly forty years. This whole place has probably been picked clean so well that you'd be lucky to find a pare of panty hose if you searched from one end to the other. Where are you from?"

"I don't understand what's going on here, but it looks like that girl and Victor are in danger."

The knife loosened.

Was it possible that she didn't know what was going on? "At any rate," he said, finally, releasing his grip on her, "this place isn't safe. Mutants breed in places like this."

"*Mutants*?"

It was possible that she was delusional. Clinging to a world which no longer existed, but she couldn't even have been born yet when the whole thing happened, and she wouldn't have survived this long without accepting reality.

He turned from her then, moving toward what was left of the entrance.

The truck was just coming around for another pass.

He ran out into the parking lot as fast as he could, pulling Victor up with one arm and lifting the girl with his other.

The truck was bearing down on them now. They made it between two cars and out the other end, just before the large vehicle smashed through them. It became obvious quickly that this would not do as cover.

"You're not going to hit me back are you?" Victor asked.

"Not at least until you can stand up straight again." Cain returned with a smile, but there was no humor in his voice. He knew why the man had hit him. It had looked bad.

"When I say go, brace yourself. I'm going to drag you to the entrance."

"I think I can walk. It's not that bad." Victor returned, unsure.

"Alright, get ready."

"We better *be* ready, here he comes," he replied, attempting not to show how scared he was.

"Go!"

Cain and Victor ran as fast as they could, Cain carrying the girl, who was no longer trying to get away, It was a miracle that they made it inside. Once back within the illusory safety of the mall, he turned to them.

"Where are you all from?"

VI

Frank pushed himself up on arms that felt rubbery, looking around the dark storage area. He tried to remember what had happened, but none of it had made sense.

He recalled hearing the bomb drop, and falling, as though the floor had vanished.

His thoughts were quickly cut off by a groan in the darkness.

Fear quickly numbed him. Although he couldn't associate that sound with any living animal he could remember ever having encountered, he recognized it just the same.

It was the sound monsters made.

The things kids feared were living under their beds. But that was crazy. He tried to assure himself that there was nothing there, or that, if there was, it surely wasn't a monster.

Then the eyes began to appear.

Instantaneously hundreds of eyes opened in the darkness as though many creatures had been awakened by his movement.

They lent a light to the room suddenly however, and he was able to see a door which was hanging diagonally, looking as though it had been smashed in at some point.

He lunged for it quickly, knowing that if he didn't make it he would die. As impossible as all of this seemed however, he knew inside that it was real. All of it. And those were monsters of some kind, as ludicrous as that seemed.

Roars of rage broke out behind him as hundreds of creatures realized that something had invaded their home, and of all things was possibly going to live to tell the tale.

Fear like no fear he'd ever felt built up in him now, threatening to stop him in his tracks. He ran as hard as he could, refusing to let paralysis set in. He'd seen it in the field and it got people killed all the time.

Who knew what these things would do to him if they caught him.

He was climbing stairs now and they were only inches from him, the whole way.

When he came to the door at the top, he let out a scream of frustration. It was locked.

An instant later he let out another cry. This time of pain, as a creature three times his size slammed its fist into him, sending him through the steel fortified door.

By all rights it should have turned him to mush, but he felt okay. Just in a lot of pain. He was not however, going to make it. That hit had broken part of his spinal column, and he couldn't feel his legs.

VII

Cain was about to get serious with questions now that they all were inside.

No questions came however, as they were all interrupted by a scream.

The place seemed to shake a second later, and there was another scream which fell short with a thud nearby.

Then there was a crash.

Cain ran instinctively toward the sound, wishing once he'd gotten there that he'd stayed away.

Not far up into the mall near Sears, a man lay in a pile of debris.

Before he could reach him, a large mutant barreled through the doorway.

"What the fuck?" Victor exclaimed behind him.

"Get the girl away!" Cain commanded, reaching over his shoulder, and pulling a rifle out. It looked roughly like a sawed off shotgun, but there was a futuristic quality to it.

He aimed and took the creature out, half of its head disintegrating in a flash of plasma from the weapon.

Then he heard the footfalls of more, half crawling, half walking up the stairs.

He aimed then, firing six times into the top of the door, where a large section of the building crashed inward, sealing it off, and trapping them below.

He then returned to the man, who didn't look like he was going to make it.

"My car."

"What about it?" Cain asked to humor a dying man.

"I have to get it from the garage in a half hour." he replied in an obvious state of hysteria. He looked as though he were struggling to say something else, then finally said, "I need ... to go home."

Victor, having returned to his side only moments before, heard all of this but said nothing. What could be said?

The man looked as if he were about to say something else, struggled for a moment to get it out, then fell silent.

Cain felt the artery in the left side of the man's neck, and found no pulse.

He was about to start asking questions, when he noticed something which had fallen from the man's pocket. As he neared it, the object became immediately identifiable. A wallet.

He picked it up swiftly, removing the man's identification.

It proved nothing. It expired two years after the war had started. The man had probably found it here on a long dead corpse.

Victor came up beside him, wishing to have a peak. "What the hell?"

"What is it?" asked Cain.

"This dude's license says it expires in Twenty Thirty."

"So?"

"So? So that doesn't make sense."

"Why not?"

"Why not? Are you nuts? Mine expires in Nineteen Ninety Six."

"What are you saying?"

"He's from the future." It was the little girl this time, standing with Heather.

A very serious look on her face.

"No," Cain started with a smile, "He's from the past, if anything. Twenty Thirty was a little over forty years ago."

"So *what*, you're saying that it's like twenty *seventy*?" Heather asked.

"Somewhere around there. I lose track."

"That's insane." Victor responded.

"What year do *you* think it is?" the little girl asked Heather.

"Well, Nineteen ninety three."

"*You*?" she asked, looking to Victor.

"Ninety five."

"Then it's *simple*," the little girl replied, "We're in the future."

Heather shot Victor a disbelieving look.

"Wait," Cain said, interrupting them from the argument they were about to get in. "It's not that unbelievable. Not this close to the rifts."

"Okay, I'll bite," Heather began after a short silence, although she looked like she was preparing to make fun of him, "What are the rifts?"

"Rips in time."

"Rips in time?" Asked Victor.

"Yes."

"In *Twenty seventy*?" asked Heather.

"Yes."

"Caused by *what*?" she asked.

"There was a war about forty years ago. Most of the U.S. didn't even know it had started until they were in the middle of it. The enemy used some kind of matter displacement bombs."

"I've never heard of anything like that." Victor objected.

"No-one had." replied Cain, "Until they were dropped however. Then the government was just full of information. They had never been tested, because they weren't sure what kind of impact it would have. Turns out it was worse than they imagined."

"So, it made a rip in the fabric of time?" the little girl asked.

"That's right. A lot of rips actually. The U.S. went nuclear on the country they thought attacked, but the attacks kept coming. I guess they never found out who was responsible. At that point it was too late, countries surrounding that one fired nukes, we fired all we had back at those countries and the war was over in a matter of hours."

"Why should we believe any of this?" asked Heather.

"Because you have no choice," Cain replied. "How else do you explain all of this?" When none of them responded, he went on. "What happened to all of you, exactly?"

"Well," started Heather, "I was walking through the mall and it was like the power went out, except I couldn't hear anyone. Like they just vanished."

"Yah," replied Victor, "Same here."

"What about you?" Cain asked, looking at the little girl. She just began crying, the memory of her father's death suddenly brought back, and clung to Heather.

"Well, what about you?" Heather asked Cain.

"Me? I grew up in the ruins, and when my family was gone, I set out to see the rifts. I would have given up, but I saw a storm of lights. At first I thought it was a spotlight, then it fanned out, and vanished, and a bad storm started. I began tracking it, and as I grew closer to the spot where it kept happening, I found that the storms were growing more and more intense. I knew I was almost upon the rifts."

"And then you found us?" asked Heather.

"Yes. And we're right in the middle of the storm."

"Well maybe we'll get sent back." Victor suggested.

"It's too dangerous."

"Why?" asked Heather, seeming angry. Wanting perhaps to believe there was still a way back home.

"There's no telling where you'd be sent. It could be during the dark ages, or further into the future. Hell it could go as far back as the dinosaurs. Or the war."

No one argued this time, but Cain wondered what it was that had made him travel all this way. Had it been for a similar idea? One perhaps inspired by a dream?

"Wait!" Victor said suddenly.

"What?" Asked Cain.

"If the war started about forty years ago, wouldn't that make it about a couple years before that guy's I. D. expired?"

"So?"

"*So*, then he might have *been* here when it happened."

"Or he could have been walking through the mall just like us." Heather answered.

"But if he was here, his car could still be in the garage."

"What's your point?" asked Cain.

"My point?" he asked, as though it should be perfectly clear, "My point is that we can't go out there, or that guy will run us down, but if there's a car in the garage at Sears, we just might have a chance."

"Well," Heather began, "he just seems to be circling the mall, so if we could just get past the parking lot we should be okay."

"Let's check out the car, before we start making plans." Victor suggested, then added, "Just don't want to get anyone's hopes up."

VIII

Victor entered the dark garage slowly.

Something was wrong here.

It didn't feel as though this place had been abandoned for forty years.

Then in the low light, he noticed a clean reflection on a car not far away. A GMC Jimmy, he noted.

Not a bit of dust on it.

'Bingo.' he thought.

He tripped on something soft just then, and cried out, as he fell forward into a wet substance around what his mind immediately identified as a body.

He fumbled around for a few seconds, finally pulling himself to all fours and inspected the corpse with his hands. He was horrified to find that only the top half of it was there as his hands quickly found their way into the man's intestines.

He couldn't have died much more than an hour Ago.

His mind wandered then back to a special he'd watched on TV about a government experiment, where they'd attempted to make an entire ship invisible.

It had actually moved it outside of known reality, and when it came back, the people on board, as well as animals were all dead. Some of them had been found half in and half out of the ship's hull.

If this man had been here when the bomb went off, he might have been moved out of his normal time stream for a second and when he came back he was half into the floor. The end effect was that he'd been cut in half.

"Everything okay?" Cain asked, from the doorway.

"Yeah." he replied, "I tripped over a dead guy."

When there was no reply he wiped the blood off onto his jeans and moved to the car. It wasn't so bad in the darkness, without a clear view of the body.

The keys were in the ignition.

*

Not far from the door, Cain noticed something. He walked toward it, curious. It was a bag which had been knocked over, spilling its contents onto the floor.

He picked it up, remembering Heather's Chinese food.

Perhaps today's miracles were not yet finished revealing themselves.

There were some supplies. It looked as though someone had been gathering things they thought would be needed either when the war had started or shortly after it ended.

Inside were flashlights, batteries, a set of hand held CB radios.

"This is almost *too* easy." he said to himself. Then the dream came back to him.

For a split second, he was back there. Fighting against the storm. A huge cathedral sat up ahead.

He pushed it away. That was a dream. He would help these people, and he'd succeed.

*

Victor turned the key in the ignition, and the vehicle roared to life.

The headlights illuminated the garage, and he got his first clear look at the mess, only a few feet away from the car. His stomach threatened to turn on him, but he reminded himself that he had seen this kind of thing hundreds of times before. The fact that it was real now, and had been on TV before meant absolutely nothing.

For the moment that line of thought seemed to work for him, but he wasn't sure how much longer.

It was then that he noticed Cain standing a few feet away, looking over the half body. A detached look of wonder and perhaps a little fear filling him.

Then his attention swiftly moved to the vehicle, and he approached, stepping over the half corpse as though it wasn't even there.

He smiled as he opened the drivers side door. "When you said you tripped over a body, I didn't think you meant a *new* one."

"What are you *smiling* for?" he asked nervously, finding nothing funny in their current situation. The bags in Cain's hands, had gone unnoticed until now.

"I found something for you." he said, retrieving the hand held radio.

"No shit." he replied, shocked. The small device sat in his hand for almost a full minute before he accepted it as real.

"I think the best route is for you to lead him to the other side of the mall while we make for the hill." he paused for a second, "Or I could do it."

"No, that's okay. I kind of figured it would be me." He got out of the car then, walking to the big overhead door, and peering out the small porthole sized windows.

"You sure you're up to it?"

"Yah," he replied, placing all his weight on the sore leg which still wasn't as bad as he'd thought it would be.

"Where will I meet up with you?" he asked, not looking at him. He knew full well that he might not make it and he didn't need to see the look on Cain's face, which he knew said just that.

"We'll be on the other side of the hill."

"I don't see a hill." Victor stated suddenly, surveying the landscape outside.

Cain was quiet for a moment, and he could feel Victors eyes on him now. He'd been thinking of the hill in his dreams. Up until this moment he hadn't realized that he'd actually thought of it as real.

"It's ... on the other side of the mall."

"You're going to take them *through* the mall?" he asked, worried suddenly. "What if you run into more of those creatures?"

"The ones I trapped in that basement, won't remain down there forever. They aren't overly smart, but they'll find a way through eventually and I'd hate to be here when they bust out." he paused for a second, seeming troubled, then continued. “I think we’ll be safer on the other side.” He turned away then, unable to look Victor in the eyes.

“What aren’t you telling us?” he asked then, taking a couple steps toward the man.

“It’s nothing important.” he replied, walking away. Once he was at the door he turned, raising the other radio. “Let us know when you’re ready.”

“Yeah, sure.”

As Cain headed back for the others, he realized that he knew exactly why he’d felt uncomfortable suddenly. He was beginning to believe that his recurring dream was in fact a vision. The storm outside wasn’t helping any. At any rate, he guessed he’d know when they reached the other side of the mall.

A chill coursed through him then, as the true reason for his worrying hit home. If the dream was a vision, why was he alone in it? *‘The answer is simple,’* he thought, *‘Because I’m the only one that’s going to make it.’*

IX

Victor watched out the small window on the overhead door. The truck was about to move out of sight.

The door was electric, but it could also be chain driven.

He’d operated this kind before. Lifting the radio to his mouth, he said, “I’m ready. Where are you guys?”

“In the food court. So far so good.”

“I’ll try and keep him on this side of the mall, but no promises.”

“Okay, we’re approaching the exit now.”

A few seconds later he had the door open and was pulling the car out into the parking lot.

No sooner had he gotten a few feet from the garage, when the truck pulled around the corner of the mall.

It stopped, waiting. Perhaps the driver couldn’t believe that he was seeing another vehicle running. Without warning, the huge truck screeched into full speed.

Victor threw his foot into the gas, and turned the wheel, sending the car spinning to the right. A second later the chase was on.

He wove through the parked cars, making it hard for the large truck to follow closely. Surely he wasn’t a match for the truck in ways of speed.

X

Cain almost had them out the doors, when a crack of light flashed across the ground right in front of them.

He reached out quickly, snatching the girl back before she could cross it.

"Wait!" he yelled.

The crack progressed onward toward the sub shop, then arched, filling that area.

As they watched, one of the employees appeared behind the counter. A shocked look of fear passing over him.

Then the light flashed again, and he was gone.

"We have to hurry." Cain shouted.

"What's going on?" asked heather.

"The storm is destabilizing the rift."

They moved on then.

"I'm in trouble." Victor said through the radio.

XI

Victor rounded the corner at full speed. Not that he had a choice in the matter however, for as he neared it, he attempted to slow himself with the brakes, but there were none.

"Shit!"

He raised the radio then, trying to keep the car steady, "I'm in trouble."

"What's wrong?" asked Cain.

"I've got no brakes, and I'm coming round to your side."

He barely made it round the next corner, and then it started raining.

"Give me a break." he pleaded.

Wind was whipping the vehicle around now.

*

"He's not going to make it," Heather cried.

They all watched as Victor screeched around the corner, finally losing control halfway across the lot and swerving into a car. The truck smashed into him an instant later.

"We can't help him. Not while that truck is still running. We have to make for the hill."

*

Victor's head hit the steering wheel, an instant before the air bag kicked in.

Darkness swam around the corners of his vision.

Then the truck hit.

A couple seconds passed, each one like an individual eternity as he fought to stay conscious.

The sound of a car door slamming, pulled him into a fully alert state.

Then the door to his vehicle was torn open, and he was yanked out onto the pavement.

He half expected death himself to be standing over him, or some body builder, but what he saw made him want to laugh, and sent a chill up his spine at the same moment. The guy was a mall cop. *'A friggen Rent-a-cop.'* he thought.

The guy reached down and lifted him into the air. He swung the instant he was in a standing position but the guy was too fast. He moved to the side and punched him in the gut.

Victor doubled over instantly. Just then the man punched him again, sending him backwards into the wreckage of the vehicle he'd been driving.

Part of the twisted metal in the nearly destroyed hatch stuck into his back and he cried out.

Stars swam around the corners of his vision, emphasized by the darkness which clouded it, and he thought this was it. He was going to pass out, and what would this freak do then?

The Mall-cop-freak was lifting him up again, when he noticed something out of the corner of his vision.

Something that looked a lot like a weapon. He reached for it as fast as he could, and got it.

A startled, dumb look passed over the freak as he realized what was happening all too late.

Victor swung hard, connecting the tire iron with the side of the crazed mall cop's head with a dull thud, and light cracking sound, as his skull no doubt caved in slightly under the blow.

The man went limp almost instantly, falling to the ground before him and it took great effort not to fall with him.

He took a deep breath and tried to steady himself.

In all the confusion he hadn't heard the sound of an approaching engine until it was upon him.

Heather pulled up in what looked to be a Pontiac Grand Am, although a model he'd never seen. Most likely from the future. He wondered then what it was that Cain had been hiding.

Surely if this area had been bombed, there would be craters and the mall would likely not even be here.

It was then that he realized the true danger of their situation. If this place was unstable and shifting in and out of sync with its correct time, it was very possible that none of them would make it out of here. All it would take is for a rift to open near one of them like it did when they were all brought here. Only this time it could be to the stone age or just before a nuke was dropped, or even worse. And let's not forget the half-mechanic back there in the garage.

"You gonna just stare at me or are you getting in?"

He snapped out of it then and reached out to the car for support.

"I'm surprised this thing started."

"I don't think it's been here long."

He didn't need an explanation. The vehicle he'd been driving looked like it had just been driven into the garage on its way back from a car wash.

"I have to show you something." Heather stated then, driving off toward the east end of the mall.

"What is it?"

He didn't need an answer for that one either.

As they neared the end of the parking lot, he saw. The city beyond was lit. It was as if the entire place was populated. Then the lights began to pulse in waves.

Some buildings faded in and out of existence.

"Oh shit!" he exclaimed as he noticed something else.

At first he only noticed the one tornado. Then it became obvious that the pitch black section which took up most of the skyline to the east was another, much bigger one. He didn't know much about them, but he'd watched a couple movies and this one was huge. If it kept coming this way, they didn't stand a chance.

It began ripping through the city, and if he hadn't seen it he wouldn't have believed it. "That thing has to be at least five miles wide."

"Oh my God."

Heather brought the car around.

XII

Cain's heart sank as he neared the top of the hill. There was no church, although the hill was identical to the one in his dream. Then he saw it. A mammoth tornado, consuming most of the horizon to the east.

"We have to get back to the mall."

The little girl gave no argument. She just followed along. Cain wondered if she would ever speak again, then decided that she would. She'd spoken once or twice earlier, and she'd been through a lot.

They were back down the hill in a few short seconds, and crossing the parking lot.

XIII

Victor and Heather were driving back toward the hill, when a crack of light shot across the parking lot at an angle.

Heather tried to swerve around it, but didn't make it in time.

"Peter," she screamed.

He turned to her, prepared to remind her that his name wasn't Peter, but it wasn't Heather.

It was someone completely different. A blond haired woman in a blue dress, gripping the wheel, her look as confused as he imagined his must be. Then in another flash of light there was no one at the wheel. The car was beginning to spin out of control.

Victor quickly reached for the wheel.

His entire arm seemed to freeze instantly.

All feeling vanished.

As he watched in horror, his arm rotted away into that of a long dead corpse.

Then the wave moved over him and his entire body fell limp. He could feel the skin rotting off the bones.

His vision clouded over, and he slipped into darkness.

"Victor!" Heather screamed.

He snapped back, fully alert, and completely intact.

"Jesus," he started, near tears, more scared than he'd ever been, "We need to get the hell out of here."

Heather swerved then, regaining control of the vehicle just short of crashing through a guard rail.

"Look." Victor exclaimed, pointing across the parking lot.

"How?" Heather asked.

XIV

Visibility had dropped considerably. Cain and the little girl waited just inside a mall entrance.

Off a short ways a figure appeared, walking toward them at a very fast pace. "Victor?" Cain asked, unable to see clearly in the storm.

The figure pulled a gun, aimed and fired before Cain could get out of the way. He pushed the girl to the ground as a bullet tore through his left arm, sending him reeling backwards.

Tires squealed on pavement and the man spun around, aiming wildly, as a car slammed into him.

He managed to get off three shots before it hit, then was thrown backwards a few feet, the gun falling from his hand.

*

Victor realized he was going to be too late when the mall cop pulled a gun.

He floored the gas pedal as hard as he could in that instant.

Just as he neared the man, he turned the gun on them.

"Get down!" he screamed at Heather, pulling her down with his right hand.

He thanked God that he'd taken the wheel only moments before.

The man fired once, missing completely. The second shot hit the windshield, but missed him.

The third shot tore into his shoulder. He cried out in pain, pressing the gas pedal even harder. A second later it was over.

The Rent-a-cop was sent flying backward, and lay a few feet from the hood of the vehicle.

Victor opened the car door, and stepped out, one hand over the wound in his shoulder.

He spotted the gun only a foot or so away.

The mall cop twitched.

Victor knelt beside the gun, watching.

The man groaned.

Without another thought he picked up the gun and walked towards him, aiming best he could and put three bullets in the man's head.

His stomach threatened to turn and a horrible feeling overwhelmed him as he realized that he'd just taken a life. He was then startled by the realization that this was only how he thought he should feel and he didn't truly care.

"So," began Heather behind him, "What do you think his deal was?"

"Well," Cain started, lifting himself up on his good arm, "Most people in his position, I think are power hungry ..."

"Control freaks," Victor interrupted.

"So what," Heather began, "He just woke up one day with no-one to control and it drove him crazy?"

"Who knows." answered Cain finally.

"Doesn't matter much now, does it?" Victor said.

The building began to creak and grown under the pressure of the winds outside.

"Is there a basement in this place?" asked Victor.

"I think it's probably full of mutants." replied Cain.

"Great." said Heather.

Just then a wall of light shot past them, and another, practically pinning them in.

"Oh shit." said Victor, prepared to run for the opening.

"No, wait." cried the little girl. "It might take us back."

"I think she's right." Cain stated, "We aren't going to make it here with a tornado that big anyway."

"Maybe he's right." Heather replied. The walls were closing in. A few feet away the car was slowly disappearing into the light.

Suddenly the dream flashed before Cain's vision, and for a second he was there again.

"I can't go with you." he replied suddenly, praying inside that he hadn't finally lost it.

"What?" Heather asked, outraged.

"I belong here."

"You'll *die* here." Victor stated.

"This is my time. I hope you make it back to yours." he said, and walked through the opening, which grew steadily smaller.

"Let him go." Heather yelled over the sounds of the closing storm, when Victor attempted to go after him. The light closed around them then.

In an instant they were in a fully populated mall, but the sounds of the storm had not disappeared.

"What the hell?" asked Victor, running past the car which people were staring at in disbelief, to the doors.

Heather and the girl followed.

Outside, the sounds of the storm were all around them, but the storm itself was nowhere to be seen. As he watched in terror, the distant city was being eaten by nothing. In its place, nature seemed to have been restored as though people had never populated this area.

He turned back to the mall, a look of realization passing over him.

"We have to get out of here."

In seconds they were back inside.

Startled shoppers watched them get inside the car. A couple seconds later they crashed through the entrance.

"I think we can make the highway if we hurry."

They drove across the parking lot at high speed, pulling onto the highway a few seconds later.

"Don't look back!" Victor told them.

As they drove away from the town, which by this time tomorrow would most likely not exist, Victor pushed a button on the radio, turning it on, and a digital display showed the date and time.

"Great." he said, "Somewhere out there, I'm eight years old."

XV

Cain made for the hill.

Every step seemed to take everything he had, but somehow he kept moving.

The winds were getting almost impossible to move in.

With any luck he'd find some sort of shelter. A cave or something.

'Or a church.' he thought to himself.

Just as he attempted to push the thought out of his mind, he saw something in the distance. It was barely visible in the storm, but it was definitely a huge building of some kind.

Why he hadn't seen it before was beyond him. A flash of lightning just then showed him that it was in fact a large Cathedral. He ran harder then, needing to reach it to prove to himself that it was actually there. "God," he said, unable to hear his own voice over the massive roar of the storm, "Please don't let me be hallucinating."

The winds were nearly knocking him down now, but it wasn't much further. The immense building loomed over him as he neared it. His hand caught onto the huge metal handle just as a gust of wind lifted him into the air and threatened to carry him away. The force from it pulled the door open. He pulled himself inside, and passed at least fifty pews, before he noticed the woman.

He'd known she was there however, just as he'd known she'd have candles lit around the alter she was kneeling before.

She turned.

"We have to get underground." he said.

The foundation of the place seemed to shake at that moment, and huge stained glass windows shattered on the other side.

"This way." she said, taking his hand. He winced as the bullet wound in his arm seemed to catch fire, but kept quiet.

There was no time to complain.

No sooner had they reached the basement, which luckily extended a couple floors beneath the earth, when the immense cathedral above them seemed to be ripped apart. It was as though two gods were battling up there.

Suddenly, no more than fifteen feet away, the wall vanished. At first he thought it was a trick of the flickering torch light. He quickly realized that he was wrong however as a wall of earth began to move toward him with incredible speed. They ran deeper into the darkened room, but fifty or so feet further, they ran into a dead end.

They were trapped.

Cain pulled the woman down and against the wall.

"Close your eyes." he told her.

The sound stopped. Cain opened his eyes to find the woman looking at him.

Their heads turned at the same time, towards where the wall of earth had been moving toward them.

Less than ten feet away, a hard packed wall of dirt and rocks sat where the rest of the room should have been.

A one foot wide gap to their right led into a much larger chamber. Just beyond that was a staircase, part of which seemed buried, but more likely was only half there.

"Be careful." Cain told her, "This whole thing could collapse at any minute. Walk slowly."

She said nothing, but appeared to be doing as he said.

A couple minutes later, they were back on the surface.

What was left of the cathedral was in ruins, but more than half of it seemed to have vanished from existence, as though it had never been built.

Without thinking, he ran for the hill he'd crossed to get here.

It only took a few seconds to reach the top.

Behind him, the woman followed.

There was no mall. No city beyond. Just wilderness. It was, with the exception of the ruined church, as though humans had never been in this area.

'And, that,' he thought, *'is probably the way nature wants it.'*

THE END

ESCAPE TO MARS

BY JOSEPH SWEET

I

Mark watched nervously out the window as the engines roared into action and the large vehicle lifted a few feet off the ground.

He wondered in that moment if he could do it. *'Not that it matters.'* he thought, *'There's no going back now.'*

Just then a slightly sarcastic voice echoed out of the tiny speakers at the front and back of the cabin. "This is your captain speaking." there was laughter somewhere just beyond that voice. Someone else in the cockpit.

"Please fasten your seat belts, be sure tables are secured in their upright position, and prepare for lift off."

More laughter.

Mark grabbed the edges of his seat.

Everything inside him wanted to stand up, to scream for them to stop. He needed to get off. Even if it did mean dying, at least he'd do it in his birthplace.

He knew deep down however that they wouldn't stop just for him. The place would be crawling with military and cops in minutes and they couldn't risk it. He was in for the duration and that was all there was to it.

The low hum over the loud speaker suggested that the microphone was still active. Somehow this demonstrated at least a little shortage of skills on the pilot's behalf and he began to hate himself for becoming a part of this.

Even a hissing sound from the vents just above him as the oxygenators came online made him jump.

Just then a voice echoed out again. This one originating from base security to the cockpit.

"Shuttle 2947, you are not cleared for take off."

This inspired only laughter from the crew which he was certain made the rest of the passengers as uneasy as it made him. He closed his eyes and began to pray that they weren't shot out of the sky.

A loud click cut security off in the middle of another word.

The rumble of the engines grew louder and louder, and the cabin felt suddenly as though they were in the middle of a great earthquake.

Cabin pressure slowly changed until his ears were about to pop, and then they took off, straight up so fast he felt glued to his seat, unable to move if he had wanted to.

They broke atmosphere in seconds. The G suit he wore alleviated some of the effects, but he knew in a couple hours he would be sore all over.

Mark allowed his eyes to open then and he looked out the porthole sized window to his left, at the stars and the increasingly smaller planet on which he had been born.

In a few days it wouldn't be the same. Nearly all its inhabitants would be dead. Except for those who had gone underground.

Those and the rich people who'd intended to use this craft.

Most likely, if conditions didn't become better in a couple years, the one's left on earth would die out as well.

The voice on the loud speaker announced that the anti inertia fields had been activated and artificial gravity sustained. It was safe to move around.

Mark un-buckled his harness, and stood up. About forty rows of seats separated him from the cockpit, and only six of them were filled. Behind him, only empty seats.

Although it seemed a waste now to transport so few on a ship built for so many, he knew that it could have been done no other way.

There had been no time to gather a big enough crew.

Not to mention that one so large would not have made it past security unnoticed.

Ahead, the door leading to the cockpit and stairs to the stasis chambers opened.

A couple of the others stood up now. One was crouched over a brown waxed paper bag, throwing up.

The man who entered was still wearing a lab coat. His name was Dr. Francis Brody. The one who'd started this all.

He cleared his throat. "Excuse me everyone. I have some bad news." he stated solemnly.

Mark's heart began beating rapidly and his skin grew cold. Surely something had gone wrong and they would have to return to earth or even worse; something had happened to the ship and they would all die.

"Now don't get into a panic," he assured them all, "It's nothing too drastic. It's just that we weren't able to get all of the supplies we'll be needing for this trip and we'll have to enter stasis early to make up for the amount of food we lost. And." he paused, a grim expression replacing his normally good natured and somewhat placid features, "A guard was killed. With any luck, they'll be too busy with all their preparations to come after us but if we get under way in the next few minutes we should be fine no matter what. As you all know, the ship refuels itself. So we'll have no trouble getting there, and if the experimental thrusters work as they were designed to, we'll all awaken in a few hours orbiting mars anyway. Now, some of you weren't in the briefing but I'm sure any questions you have will be answered by other passengers."

A young red haired woman toward the front raised her hand. Stacey, he remembered, was her name.

"Yes?" he asked with an obvious distaste for the waste of time this question and answer session would present.

He'd always been pretty anal about using time well, among most other things.

"I was just wondering, how long it will take us to get there if there's a problem with the engines?"

"The thrusters?"

She nodded.

"Well, probably a few weeks if we're to rely on standard means, plus we'll have to take into account periodic recharging of the shuttle, but it will seem as though you've awakened from a short nap when you come out of stasis."

Someone else raised his hand. A young black man of about 23.

"Yes?"

"Why do we have to go into stasis, if the thrusters don't work?"

"Well, I thought we'd just gone over that, but we don't technically have enough food to last even a week. The colony base on Mars has been presupplied with at least a years worth of packaged food for three hundred people. The supplies we brought with us, seeds and some plants, will have matured and be providing us with plenty by that point. While the oxygenators will create air even on backup power, allowing us to breathe no matter what; and the tank would allow us warmth during periodic recharges, lack of food would be the death of us, obviously."

Mark thought that the doctor's addition of the word, obviously as well as the tone in which he'd used it, were unnecessary and a bit rude. And the man who'd asked the question seemed embarrassed and unsure of himself now.

Everyone was silent.

"Well," Brody began. "If that's all, I'll have you follow me to the stasis chambers."

One by one the rest of them stood and followed him through the door to the right and up the stairs, to a room full of computers and large glass pods.

Mark pictured millions of ways this mission could go wrong. Anything from faulty wiring causing a fire while they were in stasis and unaware, to being blown up by military police for stealing the shuttle and killing a guard.

Or perhaps the ship just malfunctioning halfway there and them awakening, floating in space with no way to do a repair, and quickly running out of food. Then again maybe they'd come across a meteorite that'd smash the ship to junk, killing all on board. He tried to assure himself that the only points of danger in light speed travel was starting and stopping. According to the first tests of the ion thrusters, the ship could pass through a solid object and harm neither itself or the object, but upon slowing and accelerating, even the smallest debris could prove deadly.

"Okay," Brody started, "Now, I know a few of you are a little antsy about this part, so I'm going to show you how it works by using myself as the test subject ... Mark?"

"Huh?" he blurted being yanked from deep thought at the sound of his name.

"You're the only one who's actually worked this machinery aside from myself and the pilot, so you'll put me in stasis."

"O ... Okay." A horrible nausea passed over him right then which he hoped didn't show.

Dr. Brody stepped into one of the open glass pods and pushed a button on the inside, closing it.

Mark typed in a series of numbers and hit enter on the keyboard to the right of the doctor. Bright bluish light filled the tube for a second. Then it was back to normal and a hologram had taken his place.

Stacey placed her hand on his shoulder, startling him out of what he imagined to be pretty close to a year of his life.

"Sorry," she apologized when he practically cried out, then giggled nervously, "I was just wondering. Have you ever been in stasis?"

“Yes, Dr. Brody insists on it as part of his class. But these machines are more advanced than the ones we had in the lab and much safer.”

“How come I can still sort of see him?”

“Oh. That’s just a hologram to show that the pod is in use. The computer attached to his pod is only designed to hold the genetic information of one person. So if anyone else tried to use this one while he was in it, It’d overload and kill them both.”

He realized then by everyone’s silence that the mention of death even out of sequence with what was about to take place, had brought the subject of their own deaths to mind. “Why don’t we all get this over with?”

Stacey stepped forward quickly. “I wanna go next.” she paused, “I think if I wait much longer, I won’t be able to do it.”

“Okay.” Mark moved on to the next pod, of which there were only 34, despite the large amount of seats on the lower level, typed in a few numbers and it lit up.

Stacey stepped inside, paused for a second, doubtful; Then pushed the button, closing the pod.

In fifteen minutes everyone was in stasis, except Mark and the pilot.

He moved to the next pod, pulled up a chair which moved not on wheels, but on a track that went all around the room, keeping it mobile but still attached to the floor incase artificial gravity was lost.

He sat there for a few minutes, staring at his pod. The light inside flickered once, bringing that nervous feeling back. Somehow in a paranoid moment, that one flicker had proven the machine to be defective as far as he was concerned.

He backed away, prepared to move on to the next one, but found that he trusted this one no more than the last.

The next one seemed no better. After a few seconds he gave up and headed down to talk to the pilot, hoping that a conversation would alleviate his paranoia. And perhaps if all else failed, he would be forced into stasis once coordinates were locked by the pilot when he prepared to go himself.

*

Without even acknowledging Mark's presence at first, the pilot seemed to be in deep thought over something, bringing back a little of his prior fears that their mission was doomed.

Mark took the Copilot’s seat, and waited for something. Anything.

Finally the pilot said without looking up, "They're coming."

"Who?"

"Base security force."

The pilot pushed a small button marked Com1, and a loud voice echoed through the speakers above them.

"Repeat. Shuttle 2941. Change course and heading and return to base, or we will be forced to fire a controlled E. M. P. and board your vessel."

Thinking better of that action, the pilot reached up and pushed the button again, terminating any transmissions.

He turned to Mark then, and said, "My name's, Lieutenant Stores, Brian Stores."

"Mark," he replied, putting out his hand. "So, what's the plan Brian?"

"We've only got a minute or so, before they assume we're not going to respond and fire." he paused, "I say we plot the course, engage the thrusters and get the fuck out of dodge."

"That'll kill us."

"What do you think *they're* gonna do?" he waited but when he didn't immediately respond, added, "One of them was killed during our escape. You know what happens when a *cop gets killed*? They go after the guy that did it and *kill him*. You think Military police are any different? Besides, even if they are, do you really want to spend life in prison on a dying planet?"

"What about the anti inertia fields?"

"They won't work once we reach light speed, the field can't be sustained, because everything is momentarily reduced to a near electrical state."

"But, in theory it could keep us from being crushed. Traveling at the speed of light is not the danger. It's during acceleration and de-acceleration that we actually feel the impact."

"Go on."

"So, and maybe I'm reaching here, but if it protects us until we're almost at the speed of light and then fails, and can re-establish itself when we begin to de-accelerate, then we should only feel a split second of pressure when starting and stopping."

"I hope you're right."

"Let's find out."

The monitor before them displayed a holographic view of what was in front of the ship. One of the M. P. shuttles was beginning to move into their path.

"Do it now, before he gets in the way." Mark yelled.

Pushing a few buttons, Brian brought up a display of plot B. which showed the shuttle's course from here to Mars. Then he pressed a few more buttons, and "Confirm" began to blink across the screen in large red letters. Brian pushed a key labeled accept, and said, "hang on."

Numbers flashed on the screen, counting down from 5 ... 4 ...

Mark grabbed the straps beside him ...

3 ...

Buckled them in place ...

2 ...

Grabbed the sides of his seat ...

1 ... 0 ...

In an instant the other ships were gone, and a second later his head felt as though it would implode, his entire body forced backward into the seat, unable to move.

Then it was gone, almost weightless. Then the pressure was back again, feeling as though it would smash his bones to jelly, and then gone again.

Mars was up ahead, rushing towards them, then slowing as the ship slowed.

A loud crack, then another, and another, startled Mark, and he was certain that the ship would explode.

Then a sharp, white hot pain welled up in his arm, and he realized that he was bleeding. Something having torn right through his G-suit.

"Brian?"

No answer. He turned his head slowly in that direction, finding every inch of it difficult, the muscles in his neck feeling as though they were full of broken glass. Brian was dead. His face covered in blood, small holes covering the chest of his suit.

"Shit!"

Just then his ears started to pop, and he realized that they were losing pressure. A computerized voice from the overhead speakers announced, "Warning, Fire in Stasis Chamber ... Warning, Fire in stasis Chamber"

Un-buckling his harness, he jumped to his feet and immediately fell to the cockpit floor. Every muscle in his body felt black and blue.

"Cabins one through five losing pressure." The computer told him.

'Yah, thanks.' he thought.

The air pressure was so that he could barely breathe now.

"Warning," the computer told him, "multiple hull breaches in sector two."

Lifting himself up on his only good arm, he made it to his feet, and headed for the door.

Typing a few numbers on the keypad, he sealed off the cockpit from the rest of the ship, ran for the upstairs, tripping twice on the steps. Every movement was torture and by the time he reached the top, he was crawling.

Using every ounce of will power, he reached the upper deck.

The doors were about to be sealed shut for safety.

Standing and nearly falling again from light headedness, he reached out for the doors. Just inside was a disable mechanism and in a second he had it pulled.

The door stopped.

The chamber was ablaze.

On top of the below normal atmosphere, there was now smoke to breathe.

Thinking quickly, very close to passing out, barely able to suck in air, he went to the north wall and grabbed two oxygen masks. Each had their own bottle. Why there were only two he didn't know, but he would make do with them somehow.

The first machine was on fire, filling the air with the acrid stench of burning plastic and wires. Sparks spit forth from a gaping hole in the side.

The second machine was on fire as well, but only lightly.

Most of the units were very likely damaged beyond repair, but the second one, and the two beyond it still seemed to be intact.

Quickly pressing the correct sequence of numbers which had been drilled into his head by Dr. Brody, the machine reassembled Stacey's body.

Once complete, he opened her tube and pulled her out. Her eyes went wide as she gasped for air which was not there.

Mark placed a mask over her face and she began sucking in the oxygen gratefully.

On the other side of the room a computer system exploded, killing the electricity for most of the ship, as well as their chances of saving anyone else.

The lights died, except for what was illuminated by the fire, and artificial gravity ceased to work.

Very slowly the fire began to die out.

"We're going to die if we don't get downstairs and seal this off. Do you understand?" he mumbled through his mask.

"Uh huh."

He tried to move but he just hovered there, and managed to float off in another direction.

Stacey grabbed his arm, still holding onto the machine before her, and began pulling them along. In seconds they were in the main hallway, sealing doors behind them. Slowly the atmosphere began to grow. Emergency systems were online.

In the main passenger area, where they had started out, there were no breaches in the hull and the oxygenators were running on emergency battery power.

"What do we do?" Stacey asked nervously, knowing that most likely he didn't have the answers.

"Dunno." Mark stated.

Stacey sat in one of the passenger seats and peered out the porthole sized window at the planet they had planned to colonize. It looked different. Not red like she had seen on TV or read stories about. Large almost emerald green oceans now covered a good percentage of the surface, and though some portions of the land were still a reddish color, it looked a lot like home. All hopes of success in colonization however, seemed to be gone. The leaders of the operation were dead along with the rest of the crew, and there were only two of them left with no way to land.

"There are two E. L. V. s" Mark stated excitedly.

"What?"

"Emergency landing vehicles. There are two attached to the back of the ship.

"You just thought of this now?"

"Hey, I'm under a lot of stress here."

"You can fly, right?"

"How hard can it be," he asked in a semi confidant voice. "Can't be much harder that landing a P-1250 shuttle craft."

"*You've* flown one of those?" she asked in a sarcastic, disbelieving tone.

"Well, I've flown the *simulation*."

"*Great.*"

"Look," he started, crossing the cabin, ignoring her lack of enthusiasm toward his capability of flying, where a small screen showed oxygen and power reserve levels, "We don't have much time left until the emergency power is depleted, and the oxygenators go offline. We're going to have to stay in the tank until the E. L. V's power supply is charged. We'll be warm and we'll have oxygen. It was designed for long trips when the ship's power source needs a recharge."

She looked doubtful.

"It can hold an entire crew."

In minutes they were in the tank. The walls looked like tin foil, and with no gravity and only a bar to hold onto, they both hovered in midair.

A few minutes passed in silence.

"What about the others?"

"They're all dead."

"But, we still have to check, don't we?" She asked, very near tears.

"I saw myself that most of the machines were on fire, and the ones that weren't appeared to be in pieces."

"We have to go back." She started for the door. Mark grabbed her arm, to which she only mildly resisted, perhaps knowing as he did that there was no hope for the others.

"We can't go back up there. We'd probably end up dying ourselves. It's not worth the risk. If we don't make it to the surface then what was all this for?"

She remained silent.

"Shit!" Mark blurted suddenly.

"What?"

"The key to start the E. L. V. is around the pilot's neck."

"Great."

"I'll go get it. Wait here."

Stacey wanted to argue. It was obvious that he was in a lot of pain, but perhaps with no gravity, he'd be alright. The entrance to the tank had a sealed corridor, so that the environment outside wouldn't conflict with the one inside.

The wall in the adjoining hall was lined with space suits.

In seconds he was at the door to the cockpit. Every muscle fought against him. He almost lost his grip and floated off twice but managed to get the door opened. The cockpit was a mess. Ice crystals covered everything, and most of them around the pilot were red.

His face was nearly destroyed, and the flesh appeared to be frozen solid.

Mark attempted to unzip the man's jacket, but all that he succeeded in doing was breaking a frozen chunk of it off, along with part of the zipper.

He began frantically ripping at the fabric then, which continued to break until the key was revealed. His sore arms, ready to give way at any moment.

His fingers were almost refusing to do what he wanted them to through the gloves of the suit.

Rather than trying to move the pilot's head, he just yanked the key backward and the chain broke.

Just then, the artificial gravity came back online.

He hit the floor instantly.

With each passing second the gravity seemed to get stronger and stronger, Until he felt that he couldn't move another inch.

He began to crawl.

Finally after a couple of minutes, his body began to fail him, and he collapsed. As he lay there, he wondered why he hadn't just stayed on earth to die.

Then just inches away, a foot appeared.

He used every ounce of strength left in him to look up.

Stacey had come to help him.

He lost consciousness.

*

Perhaps an hour had passed when he awoke in the E. L. V. on the Copilot's side.

Stacey was nowhere to be found. He attempted to move but to no avail. For the moment his body had given up in favor of restful healing.

He wondered then how long that would take. Maybe months.

Just then there was a hissing sound of the pressurized door opening in the bottom of the small shuttle.

It was Stacey. She seemed to be dragging something.

A few seconds later she sat in the pilot's seat.

"I Thought you couldn't fly?" he managed in a little more than a whisper.

"Well," she began with a hint of a smirk, "I've flown the sims too. Didn't seem worth mentioning before."

He gave a weak smile.

She pulled back on a lever which released them from the ship, and the view before them changed from that of the ship and part of mars, to swimming stars which made him sick to his stomach.

A second later the engine roared into life and they were on their way.

"I have to say it." she began then, "I had no idea that terraforming had come this far."

"I know," he said weakly, "It looks inhabitable now."

On their approach Mark was certain there was plant life down there at the least, and that was supposed to be years away.

They entered the atmosphere and their vision was distorted by fire.

When it cleared, they appeared to be in a desert.

"Nope," she said, "Regular uninhabited Mars."

Then the engines failed.

She pulled back on the stick, trying to bring the nose up, but was unsuccessful in preventing a crash landing.

Just before they would have hit, she got the nose up enough so that they coasted along the ground.

Something flew by them that couldn't have been just then.

"Was that a *Camper*?" Asked Mark, bewildered.

"Couldn't have been."

Then they went over a cliff and into a town.

A regular everyday, seemingly American town on Mars.

Neither of them could speak as this unusual event came to pass.

Then they finally slammed into pavement and skidded to a stop in the middle of a street.

Mark wanted to make a comment about a sign post up ahead, say they had entered the twilight zone, but he was fighting a losing battle to stay conscious. As he faded into darkness, he thought, *'I'll have to remember this when I wake up. What a dream.'* Then he was gone.

Stacey attempted to awaken him but he only moaned.

His body would now require much sleep no doubt to heal.

She looked out then in wonder at the town, and as she did, a bird flew by overhead.

There was oxygen.

Quickly, without thought, she opened the emergency exit and jumped down onto the pavement below.

'What a shame,' she thought, *'to have come all of this way only to have no-one but an unconscious person to share the experience with.'* She sighed then, looking around at the houses which seemed to have been abandoned for years, and her blood ran cold.

Everyone here was dead. But how could all of this be? A town on Mars? And then she realized. The only explanation. Einstein's theory on time travel.

She didn't know all of the details but it had something to do with traveling at the speed of light. Her and Mark had somehow moved a great deal into the future.

"They made it here, but they all died."

More people from earth had no doubt come here eventually, but something had killed them. She wondered then if it had been a disease, but it was a little too late to worry about that now. What safety there had been, she'd discarded when the emergency hatch was opened, letting in oxygen, and whatever germs were in the air.

Her thoughts ran then to the stasis pods, which she had gone back to while mark slept. Nine of the data drives she'd been able to salvage from them. And if even one of them still held all of its information intact, there was a possibility of saving that person.

The sun came out from behind a cloud just then and she found it renewing the hope which had slowly been draining out of her since she'd been brought out of stasis.

Whatever had killed everyone, seemed for the time being to be no danger to her and Mark. And if things continued that way, maybe everything would be alright.

"We made it." she stated confidently.

HELL 101

BY JOSEPH SWEET

Francis crouched behind the window. How he had made it this far was beyond him. He knew he should try and run while he could, but the right thing to do was to stand his ground and take these men out. To be true to himself and be the man his father had taught him to be.

The posse was across the street. As far as he could tell, two hid behind a horse trough and the other one was out in the open. That one was the leader.

They'd rode into town the night before.

Then there were six of them. All those who'd stood up had been shot down one by one. The ones who surrendered were shot as well.

Looking around for anything he could use, he spotted a revolver inches from a dead man's hand. He grabbed it, opened the chamber, separated the spent shells from the unused bullets. Chances were that they would do him no good in his revolver, but he kept them just incase.

The man had been the Sheriff. A thought occurred to him then, and he took the man's badge from his shirt and put it on his own. *'A lot of good this badge did him.'* he thought, but left it there anyway. If there was anyone left in this town willing to stand up and take charge, he guessed it would have to be him.

Time was running out. There was another window on the other side of the room.

He threw the empty revolver through that one and stood at his.

All three men stood and began firing at the broken window and he took two of them there. One in the chest and the other in the head. His father - rest his soul - had not taught him to miss.

The third man however, turned on his first shot and fired five times, fanning the hammer as quickly as the chambers could spin.

He'd gotten the first man without taking any bullets himself, but on the second shot, he took one in the left shoulder.

He went down hard, the wind forced out of his lungs so quickly and forcefully that he feared they would collapse and he'd be dead right here.

He could tell the moment he moved his arm, that there was no irreparable damage to his shoulder. It had been a clean shot.

Most likely the man who'd shot him didn't know how bad the wound was however, so he waited there on the floor, Bleeding.

"Come on out hero." cried the stranger. He was testing. Waiting to see if he'd killed him or not.

"It's just you and me now. Come out and fight me like a man, coward!"

At this he almost stood, but he realized something else.

He was getting closer, stalling.

Perhaps waiting to bust in at any moment, and make sure he finished the job.

Francis crawled to the other side of the door.

Most likely he would expect him to be near the window.

No more than a split second later the door was kicked in.

The stranger spun instantly toward the spot where he'd expected him to be and then wildly toward Francis when he wasn't there. This was all of the distraction that he needed and he put a bullet in his head as he turned.

The man went down quickly, firing a couple of shots and then spasming wildly, as the life drained out of the hole where his nose had been in one dark shade of red.

Francis stood, staggered slightly and made his way to the door. He needed to see no more of the dead man.

He wasn't squeamish, but he'd seen enough death today. Hell, enough for a lifetime.

Standing there looking out at the street littered with bodies, he took a deep breath and sighed. It was over.

Somewhere close by, there was the thunderous bang of a revolver and a hollow thud.

Then darkness. As it enveloped him, he thought, *'One of'em lived.'* but nothing mattered.

Francis awoke, as if from a deep sleep, wiping the drool from his desk, and off his chin. A pile of school books sat next to his head. "Wow," he thought at the vividness of the dream, and then laughed at the thought of having been a gunslinger in the old west.

Then he looked around the classroom. There were many people sleeping and some who appeared to be awakening just then.

'Must be a substitute today,' he thought. Then another thought occurred to him. *'I graduated from high school almost fifteen years ago.'* Surely this was a dream.

He tried to remember the last thing he had done, but was at a loss. The gunslinger dream seemed as real as anything else he could remember.

'Okay,' he thought, grabbing the pen which sat on his desk and a pad of paper from the pile of schoolbooks, and started to write his name.

Francis MacDougall, was what he almost finished writing, and then stopped at the first letter of the last name. Another name seemed to be floating there.

Michael Sathers. He didn't write it however, because just as he began to get the pen near the paper another one came to him.

Frederick MacDonald.

He put the pen down.

When he tried again to remember the last thing he had done, several bits and pieces of stories that didn't intermingle began to play themselves out in his head.

In one he was on a bus and a car was coming around the corner out of turn. He'd tried to yell for the bus driver to hit the brakes, but it was too late. The gunslinger story seemed real too and another one about a plane which was shaking. Strange clear plastic masks were dangling before him. Everyone had been screaming.

"I've lost my mind." he said aloud, but barely more than a whisper.

"You are probably all confused." A teacher at the front of the room announced. He had a dark brown mustache and beard, which was graying around the edges. And Ice blue eyes, which just didn't seem natural on a face like his. It was like the guy that played Freddy Krueger wearing ice blue contacts.

Something just made it seem way too wrong. Then again, a second later he couldn't remember who Freddy Krueger was, let alone who the guy was that played him. And he wondered where the thought had come from. This was beginning to shape up like one of those dreams where you seem to know everything about a life that didn't exist, but you don't know it didn't exist until you woke up.

"I assure you," the teacher continued, "I'll have some answers for you soon, but you really must stay in your seats until you're able to calm your minds and make some sense of this for yourselves."

He returned to a desk on the left front of the room.

The green chalkboard announced that his name was Mr. Kirkland.

Francis, he decided to call himself for the moment, even though his mind immediately screamed a hundred other names at him. 'Michael ... Frank ... David ...' until he wanted to scream in frustration. He was tempted to raise his hand, but what if he was just suffering a mental breakdown, and he was in school; a class that he was supposed to be in, and he just couldn't tell reality from fiction anymore. How embarrassing would it be to raise your hand and ask where you were or who you were. *'Hey teacher, am I really a gun slinging cowboy, or a college student? Or maybe a doctor?'* Obviously there was no real way of asking such a question without seeming purely insane, and he wondered if he was in fact having a much more lucid version of one of those crazy dreams that just didn't make sense.

A man at the front of the class stood up and walked to the teachers desk.

It was impossible to hear what they were saying even though they couldn't be more than a few yards away. It was as though there was an invisible sound barrier between them and Francis's seat. Seconds later the man walked to the classroom door and out into the hallway beyond.

Something seemed wrong about the teacher, but he kept trying to tell himself that he didn't really know anything about the man, and as such, had no basis by which to judge him.

'Maybe this is just a dream.' he thought at that moment, and laid his head down.

Moments later he must have fallen asleep. When he awoke there were only a few people left in the room and as he looked around, one of them raised his hand and the teacher motioned for him to come to the desk.

He listened carefully to the sound the man's feet made on the hard tiled floor as he walked across the classroom, and although his speed did not change and he appeared to walk no softer; the sound died no less than a desk away.

Hair raised on the back of his neck. *'Something is wrong here.'* he thought, then assured himself that it was just imagination.

He noticed the teacher watching him then. He couldn't quite explain what it was that was wrong in that gaze.

Then he remembered something.

His name was Everett. That was the last one.

'What do you mean, last one?' he asked himself immediately.

"Your last incarnation." The teacher said, standing over him now, as if he'd been honing in on his thoughts.

"As in past life you mean?"

"Exactly."

"So, what now? This is the new one?"

He just looked at Everett with something akin to pity.

"Am I dead?"

"You're *talking* to me aren't you?" the man asked.

Everett wasn't sure how to take that. Did he mean that since he was talking to him he was obviously *dead*, or that since he was talking he *couldn't* be dead?

"That second one." the Teacher responded to his mental question.

"Well then have I lost my mind? Am I speaking to you from my delusional world while in a therapy session or something, or am I in a coma..?"

"You are in the process of crossing over, but although the body you lived in is dead, you are alive, otherwise you wouldn't be able to talk to me right now."

When Everett didn't respond right away, he continued, "It's a little much to absorb, but when you are ready to accept and talk about it, you can come over to my desk."

With that he walked back across the room.

Everett looked around to the other three in the room, who'd been watching him talk to the teacher, but they immediately looked in another direction, as though embarrassed to have been eaves-dropping.

He wondered then if that's what they'd been doing. So far when people talked to the teacher, he'd been unable to hear the conversation. He didn't know, but he'd be willing to bet it was the same case here.

'Jeez,' he thought, *'Listen to yourself. Even in the afterlife, you're still judging people.'*

With that he decided to give the man another chance, and he walked to the desk.

There was something then which seemed to take him over. A feeling of losing control, and he fought it. After a couple seconds it passed and he felt better.

"Are you ready?" the teacher asked.

"Um, Yeah." he said.

There was a grin on the teacher's face now that he didn't like, but he tried to convince himself that it was just in his head.

"I want you to repeat after me."

"Oh, Okay." he said, finding it more and more difficult to talk."

"I."

"I."

"Everett Michael Peterson."

"Everett Michael Peterson."

"Do solemnly swear."

He paused at this one. Did he have to take an oath when he died, in order to move on?

"Do solemnly swear." the teacher repeated, sounding a slight bit agitated.

"Do solemnly swear." he heard himself say as though from a great distance.

"Allegiance to he who was persecuted and outcast, but is righteous."

"Allegiance to he ..."

He noticed something then. Perhaps the teacher was unaware, but someone's fingers were laying on the floor near his desk. He tried to look at them without being obvious. And there, not far from the fingers ... Was that a *whole hand*?

"Everett?" the teacher questioned. "Am I losing you?"

Everett didn't respond. Then he noticed the knife in the teachers left hand.

Had it been there the whole time?

"Mister Peterson?"

He still didn't reply, noticing now that the knife had blood on it and that one of the teacher's fingers was missing. Appearing in fact to just have been cut off.

'Well if he's only missing one finger, then who's are those on the floor..?'

Before he could ponder the thought much longer, he saw with growing horror that the missing finger had begun to grow back.

The teacher, obviously still unaware that he had seen these things, said, "Mister Peterson, perhaps you should take your seat if you aren't ready yet."

"Yeah sure," he said and then he looked into the teacher's face and saw that he wasn't half as human as he had previously looked. He still had the beard but his face was disfigured and as he watched, the demon began to cut off another finger as though it were nothing. A sly smile passed over him as he did so, and Everett thought, *'He's doing it to maintain the image of being normal. The pain helps him stay calm and hide his true form.'*

Slowly he began to back away from the desk.

"What's wrong with you boy?" the teacher asked, seeming to have realized that something had changed in him now.

"No. Nothing." he lied. "Just not ready." He turned to the class then of only three other than himself, and realized that they were all being misled; and all of the people in the class with the exception of the four of them had been fooled.

"We have to get out of here." he told the class, realizing how crazy he sounded in that instant, but unable to do anything about it.

When everyone just looked at him, he continued, "He's lying to us. We're not going to move on. He tried to get me to take an oath, and swear allegiance to he who has been persecuted and outcast but is righteous. Whoever that is, it doesn't sound like an oath you would take to get into heaven."

The teacher grabbed him by the back of the neck, having stood and gotten to that position in the room so fast that the other three in the class gasped in shock simultaneously as he appeared to have just materialized in that spot.

He was spun around and made to face the demon.

"Look at him." Everett pleaded with the rest of the room.

Two of them stood, and began to back toward the door.

The demon made no move to stop them. They had seen through him.

Everett punched the demon in the stomach as hard as he could, but nothing happened. Then he kicked the smiling bastard in the nuts and the grin faded, as he doubled over in pain.

He ran then, grabbing the arm of the only guy in the room who had not already gotten out of his seat of his own free will.

In seconds they were in the hallway, which seemed like a normal school hallway with lockers from the twenty first century.

"Which way?" one of them asked.

"Just run." Everett replied and began running to his left.

They were right behind him.

Then he lost one of them. The man was simply there one minute and gone the next.

The other two didn't even seem to have noticed.

Then he watched as one of the other two turned slightly and vanished into one of the lockers.

The last two of them stopped there, staring at the spot where the guy had vanished, and this one realized for the first time that the other had gone now as well and there were only the two of them left.

“I don’t understand.”

“What do you see?”

“What do you mean, what do I see?”

“I see a school hallway with lockers.”

The man looked at him then, obviously scared, “I see a long corridor with Corinthian columns.”

Everett had no idea what Corinthian columns were, but he envisioned something similar and thought he had the right idea.

“Okay, we’re obviously not in the same place, we can just see each other for some reason.”

“That doesn’t make sense.”

“I ...” he started, just when an earth quake hit. And parts of the walls began to crumble. Not far down the hall in the opposite direction than the one they were headed in, the floor began to give away. Very quickly the collapsing floor dissolved into a seemingly unending darkness, which moved toward them with an unnerving speed.

“Run.” Everett, screamed, “If we can’t stay together, at least run,” he said, as his feet carried him faster that he thought they had ever done before.

The other one was gone so fast that he must have run through a wall that wasn’t there for him, like the others.

Everett ran as fast as he could, but the gap grew closer, and then he noticed that up ahead another gap was coming toward him.

Not too far ahead on the left was a staircase. He made an even harder run for it and began up just as the ground gave way beneath them.

The stairway began to crumble then too, but he was near the top, and as his section gave way he jumped and caught the top step.

As he struggled not to fall into the abysmal darkness below, a hand took hold of his, and a beautiful young woman pulled him up.

He found himself in a group of people who’s spirits seemed high, and he quickly realized that the ones who hadn’t yet noticed him were talking about god.

‘Maybe I’m in the right place now.’ he thought, and started to let his defenses down.

Things should be alright now.

Then he saw the teacher. The man from the classroom below. And as someone walked by him, he vanished.

He stepped backwards.

"Are you okay?" the woman before him asked.

When he shifted his vision in another direction, he noticed that two people were making their way to him now through the crowd.

Then off to the left, two more. One of them was the teacher, only he looked normal now. He began to back away, but realized that there was nowhere to go that way except the abysmal black nothing behind him.

He ran for the door on the other side of the classroom, yelling that this was not what they thought it was. No one appeared to pay him any attention. As far as they cared, they had reached the place they were supposed to be, but he knew they were wrong.

'No time.' he reminded himself, and made his way out into the hallway, running as fast and hard as he could; he expected the floor to give way beneath him at any second, and hear evil mocking laughter as he fell into an endless dark pit.

Instead everything actually grew brighter and brighter until he could no longer make out any details and he was just in light.

Then he awoke.

The hospital room was crowded with people who were being told to step out. A doctor and a couple of nurses were leaning over him. One of the nurses gently pushed him back down onto the bed. "Welcome back." she said with a warm smile. "For a while there we didn't think you were going to come out of it."

"Out of what?" he asked her, beginning to feel as though he would pass out again.

"You have been in a coma for a week."

He drifted off to sleep again, a smile on his face as he did so. Everett Peterson was alive. Later he would forget about the demon, but he retired early from teaching that year, because he couldn't bare being in a school environment anymore. Something about it unnerved him.

THE END

FEEDING TIME

BY JOSEPH SWEET

Greg sat in the large picture window of his apartment, looking down on the streets below. He was vaguely aware that someone in a nearby building may be able to see him and think him a peeping tom, but he didn't care. He was having trouble sleeping, which usually meant he was writing, but tonight he wasn't able to do that either.

On nights like this, sitting in the window watching the occasional passing car or pedestrian seemed to calm him and before he knew it he usually found himself waking up to the morning sun with a cramped neck and sore body, but at least he'd finally gotten some sleep.

Just then a woman came into view, walking quickly, eyeing the shadows for only milliseconds at a time. Eyes down the rest of the way. Trying not to see anyone or anything.

A car passed her and slowed to a crawl.

Stopped.

Greg's heart seemed to freeze in his chest. Something was about to happen. Something bad, he just knew it. He didn't know if there was a way that a person could drive a car that seemed menacing, but the way this vehicle slowed and stopped was almost predatory in nature.

He tried to assure himself that the person in the car lived nearby or was just new in town and was stopping to ask directions. Inside he knew better. As the driver's door opened, the building fear only intensified.

He left the window and headed for the door, reminding himself the entire way how stupid this was.

"This is nuts."

He was down three flights of stairs in a few seconds. As he neared the front entrance, the car came into view, and he ducked into the shadows to watch.

A man in his thirties, short black hair, clean shaven, in blue jeans and a black t-shirt was standing over the trunk, shifting something around inside. Every couple of seconds he looked around as though making sure no one was looking, then went back about his business.

A woman's leg fell outward, dangling over the edge of the trunk. The man quickly put the leg back inside and closed the hatch carefully, swinging his head around in all directions one last time to ascertain whether or not this last had been spotted by anyone.

Greg immediately backed against the nearest wall. "Oh god." he breathed.

A car door closed outside and he looked again to see the vehicle pulling back out onto the road.

'Gotta stop him.' he thought before he could question this action. He was outside in an instant, running, but the car was already halfway down the block.

He ran faster, but the vehicle turned left at the corner.

Thinking quickly, not wanting to lose them, he ducked in between a fence and the side of another apartment building, through the alleyway behind this one. He cut across a back lot and ran the length of another where he came out on the street the car had turned onto.

"Shit."

It was turning at the next corner.

He crossed the street and ducked in between two buildings, across a lawn and onto the next street.

There he just caught sight of the vehicle, turning into a driveway.

"Gotcha." he said triumphantly to the night.

The car pulled into a garage.

He walked down the sidewalk at a very fast pace, wanting to retain the image that he was power walking in case he was spotted. But as he neared the house he saw that the garage door was closing.

The house was encased on either side by a factory and an office building with no windows on that side, leaving the back yard completely walled in. The only way to see into it was to be in it or in the back side of the house.

The garage lights went out and he crossed the street.

As he entered the driveway he could see the man exiting the far side of the garage through a small door. The woman was draped over his shoulder.

Greg ran around the back side of the garage, listening for any sound.

All he heard was footsteps on grass. He ducked in behind some bushes.

"This is nuts." he reminded himself. The man walked across the back yard to what appeared to be a small but elaborate Stonehenge recreation. In the center was an altar draped in red silk. He laid the woman upon it with her head hanging off the far end, arms on either side.

Slowly he undressed her.

Just when Greg was about to become involved, the man stood and walked away toward the house, entering through the back door. He seemed to be rushing to get inside as though he feared something out here.

Certain that he'd been spotted, Greg thought about running.

"I can't just *leave* her." he whispered, reprimanding himself. Then he thought, *'To hell with curiosity, it's your conscience that can get you killed.'* He began running toward the woman, sure that at any moment he would be shot.

When he reached her, he attempted to awaken her but to no avail. She was out cold.

"Hey, wake up."

A gunshot startled, and nearly deafened him. The stranger was standing just outside the back door holding the weapon.

"Are you crazy?" the man asked.

'Apparently,' he thought, but said nothing.

"Get out of here before you kill us all."

Just then the ground began to shake.

"Leave her and get out of here before it's too late." he pleaded, near hysterics.

The rumbling grew louder and the tremors rose to the level of a small earth quake.

The stranger ran back into the house.

Greg took off his sweater, covered the woman and lifted her into the air.

She began to wake up then.

"Where am I?"

"I'm going to get you out of here. Can you walk?"

"Yeah," she stated, although it came out as little more than a whisper.

He helped her to her feet.

The ground continued to shake as though the big one had finally hit, though not in California as everyone had thought. But right here in good old Watertown, N.Y.

'What are the odds?' he wondered, *'All of this happening, and an earthquake at the same time.'*

But he knew that the question was willfully ignorant.

Deep down he was aware that something was coming.

He just didn't want to believe it.

"No!" the stranger cried, outside once more, running toward them.

As they left the stone circle the earth-quake stopped.

The stranger stopped as well.

"No." he whispered. All hope seemed to have abandoned him.

A manhole near the center of the stone circle which he had not noticed until just then, opened. They all stood watching in horror.

Midnight black tentacles shot forth lightning quick from the manhole, slithering through the grass towards them and the stranger with a preternatural speed.

An inhuman gurgling sound, embedded within a hellish shriek issued forth from the hole as well which made Greg's blood go cold.

"Run!" Greg ordered, feeling a fear building inside him that he only just now realized could exist outside of the worst childhood nightmares. "Now!"

They ran toward the factory where a metal ladder scaled the side of the building. Trying not to look back. Not wanting to see what was attached to those tentacles.

The stranger screamed in agony behind them.

"Don't look back," he told her. The shrieking sound had stopped.

"Oh, Gods No!" The stranger pleaded behind them.

Horrid screams echoed out from the property below such as one would expect to hear in a sixteenth century torture chamber then, meshed with wet, meaty, ripping sounds and the screams faded into a sickly gurgling, then silenced.

They scaled the side of the building in minutes, then stood looking down on the yard. By the time they had reached the top, the manhole had returned to its place and everything was silent again. The stranger was nowhere to be seen.

"It's over." she said.

"Yes, but what worries me, is who's going to feed that thing when the time comes again? And what will it do if no-one comes."

They looked at each other for a moment then, an uncontrollable shiver moving through them both in that instant.

They were alone in this. No-one would ever believe them.

All they could do is wait and hope that when feeding time came again, the creature didn't remember and come for them.

LAST TRAIN

BY JOSEPH SWEET

*

For a moment, Harold was unsure where he was or how he'd gotten there. He could sense his wife beside him and knew that they'd been standing in the same place for quite some time.

There was a great hiss behind them. And a SSHH SHHH SHH sound, growing faster and faster.

Harold turned, suddenly remembering that they had been on a train.

It was moving much too fast for him to catch it at his age.

Maybe at fifteen or even twenty, he'd have ran after and jumped onto the platform, but at the age of sixty eight - whether he liked to admit it or not - he would run out of breath or have his legs give out on him before he got up even one fifth of the speed which would be required to catch it.

"Harold?" Betty asked, appearing to still be in the daze from which he was just now beginning to recover. Her breath was visible on the cold morning air and Harold began to realize how chilly it actually was out here. It was as though he'd not only just awakened but just arrived here.

"Yeah?" he asked, not really wanting to talk. Wishing rather to get a better idea of their surroundings, and remember how it was exactly that they'd gotten here. The answer was floating there, just beyond his reach, waiting for him to remember it, but he couldn't grasp it.

"Did we *miss* it?" she asked, her trembling voice just shy of panic.

He suddenly realized that he didn't have a clue as to how he could answer that. Had they missed what? It came suddenly that they had been traveling, but to where?

Surely his wife was suffering from the same loss of memory as him, but even at his age he refused to suffer the embarrassment of letting her know that he didn't have the answer. Not to mention where they were now, or how they had gotten there. At least he could remember his name. *'This is how it starts, isn't it?'* he thought. *'Alzheimer's.'*

He looked around for the first time then and noted that the surroundings were not at all familiar. It was a train station like many of its sort. But he had never been here in his entire life. At least not that he could recall.

Mountains surrounded on all sides, all of which were covered in snow. It seemed not only odd, but frightening that he couldn't remember stepping off the train, and he was sure in that moment that he was dreaming the entire thing.

And then a vision caught him and he was lost in it. He had never been one to day dream, but this one was vivid as hell. He was on a train. Yes! On the way to visit his brother Frank.

Frank's wife had died and they'd come to console him.

He'd stood because several people were getting out of their seats to see something out the left windows.

As he left his seat however, the train rocked and as normally happened in vivid dreams; Just as he was on the verge of what appeared to be a life changing discovery, he was yanked backward, forgetting just enough that it didn't seem to make sense.

"We missed it didn't we?"

"Yah." he said, mainly to shut her up, and tried to go back to his thoughts, but she wouldn't let up.

"We should go inside and find out when the next train is."

'That's it,' he thought. *'We missed a connecting train or something.'* "Okay." he replied simply.

"There aren't any mountains in Florida." a voice spoke up in his head just then.

"*You,* shut the hell up." he whispered, and then realized it had been loud enough to hear.

"What?" Betty asked, seeming not to have heard the words.

"Nothing."

They began walking without thought. It only occurred to him as they reached the door, that train stations usually had people walking around, waiting for loved ones or the next train. There was no one to be seen here.

A chill began to slide casually down his spine as they walked inside and he wondered if they ought to be doing this.

At that moment however, he felt as though he was being watched from somewhere out here and his paranoia had him convinced that there was some danger to just standing around.

Once inside, it became obvious that the place was abandoned.

Dust and cob webs littered the place. There were no lights and apparently no people either.

'Why would a train let people off at an abandoned station?' he wondered.

There would be no answer however and he knew it, so he turned, and despite his paranoia, walked further into the building.

"Harold?"

"What?" he asked, mildly agitated.

"Where are we?"

The look in her eyes was that of a person who was about to become hysterical.

He walked back to her, taking her in his arms, "It's okay honey, we just missed the connecting train." He had no idea if that were true, but it felt right.

Suddenly there was the sound of movement from across the station and he had that feeling that someone was watching again.

He let go of her and asked her to stay there, and he walked deeper into the small, unlit building.

A feeling of tiny insects crawling over the entire length of his spine grew stronger, until he felt that he would begin to shake uncontrollably. There was something here and it was watching him.

'That's foolish old man.' He told himself. *'Just letting yer imagination have its way with you.'*

There was movement off to the left. Out of the corner of his eye he caught it. Fluid movement, like a black sheet caught in the breeze, but moving with purpose, followed by a thin raspy sound. It was like thousands of dead leaves crushed under an enormous foot, then blown away on a light breeze.

Fear threatened to paralyze him, but he managed to turn in that direction, only to find nothing but a cobweb infested train station. But it had been there. He was certain about that.

"Harold?" Betty called, causing his heart to nearly leap out of his chest.

"What?" he asked, angry now. Startled out of at least a couple years of his life, and at his age those years were more important than ever.

"I thought I heard something."

There was that sound again, which seemed to make the very marrow of his bones solidify, and his blood run cold, and then Betty screamed.

He spun in her direction instantly, but was only fast enough to see a black shadowy blur, as something disappeared beyond the doors into the bright sunny day beyond.

There was only a moment of fear, and then it was gone, replaced by concern for the woman he'd spent the last thirty years with. And he was running.

As he neared the doors, they slammed shut, and he ran into them at full speed. His head hit the hard tiled floor as he fell backwards, and bright lights danced around the corners of his vision, but he managed to stay conscious.

The world threatened to spin out of focus as he reached his feet, and he realized in disbelief that there was a chain and a large padlock holding the door closed.

He took the lock in his hand and gave it a hard pull, but there was no way for him to get the door opened. His heart sank in his chest, as he realized that there was nothing he could do for her.

There was another scream outside just then, and he began lunging at the doors with all of his strength, but to no avail. He looked around desperately, very close to collapsing, for anything that he could use to aid him, but there was nothing.

The chairs were bolted to the floor securely and the trash cans that most likely used to be here, appeared to have been removed long ago.

In despair, he sunk to the ground, leaning against the door. The screams had faded now but had seemed to have continued until she'd been dragged too far away for him to hear them. He began crying then.

*

Harold awoke suddenly in darkness.

Light was still spilling through the doorway, but it was the light of a full moon now.

'The door!' he thought.

It was open now, and he was leaning against a post not far away. He was certain suddenly that he'd been leaning against the door, but there was no time to think about it now.

He ran out into the night, surprised at the energy he had now. Most days lately he was lucky to make it from his living-room chair to the bathroom without being out of breath.

"Betty?" he called, but knew there would be no response.

Something passed behind him so quickly he only caught a blur as he turned, and then it was gone. He ran back toward the building, but stopped abruptly when he heard Betty say his name.

As he turned back, the creature stopped just a few yards away.

Harold got a good look at it this time. Its shape seemed to be molded by the wind in some places, fading in and out of existence in others, but very clearly a man shaped figure, and most obviously Death himself.

It raised something that it had been holding at its side then, and Harold saw light slide across a reflective surface that wasn't entirely in this world.

There was no light in the building behind him to reflect either. It pulled the scythe back at an arc, obviously preparing to attack, and Harold backed away and into the station slowly.

It lunged at him with inhuman speed, and he just barely missed being sliced in half as he dove through the doorway, and back outside to get away.

He hit the ground with a thud, rolling into a crouch.

Somehow through it all, he marveled that his bones didn't protest, his muscles hadn't threatened to give out on him. It was as though he'd gone back twenty five or thirty years.

It came at him again.

He ran back into the station.

Once inside, he found the chain laying nearby. The lock, which had been there earlier, was missing now however.

He quickly secured the door, using the chain as best he could, and slowly backed away from it. Surely it wouldn't hold long against that creature.

"It's no use Harold," his wife said to him from outside the door, and then he knew that he wasn't suffering from Alzheimer's, or having a mental breakdown.

Most likely he'd already long since *had* the breakdown, and was in a mental hospital somewhere, imagining all of this. Things of this sort surely didn't happen in the real world.

Perhaps he'd had a stroke.

The sudden certainty that this was all in his head, didn't alter his fear of the situation, however, and he began to look around for another place to hide.

Something slammed against the doors so hard then that they almost opened and he found himself running for the bathrooms, but once at the doors, he realized that there was no way to lock them.

A short ways off to the left there was a small office.

Another crash at the door assured him that it wouldn't be long now.

Once inside the office, with the door barricaded, he backed into the corner.

"Harold, open the door." His wife said, nice as could be; as though death himself wasn't standing in the shadows just outside, waiting to take him. As though he would realize upon doing so that he was just being foolish.

That raspy sound again, like leaves blowing across cement, was almost like laughter this time. As if a being made of shadows and smoke was trying to laugh with its smoky vocal chords, and all it could produce was this whispery demonic chuckle.

"Stop it!" he screamed at the door.

With more substance this time, a deep menacing laugh came from the darkness of the lobby. "Oh Harold." Said his wife, as though pitying him.

"Stop it!" he demanded, putting a hand to each ear.

The laughing simply grew louder, until his hands could provide no comfort to his ears any longer.

At this point he realized that the ticket windows looked in on this room, and he knew that he had made a mistake. It would take nothing for that creature to break through the glass and come in here.

Standing, he tried to decide if he could make it back out the door again, if it did crash through. What he saw in the glass however, stopped all thoughts of danger and escape.

His reflection showed, not a sixty eight year old man, but Twenty at the most. His face, unworn by time. He reached out toward the glass to make sure that it was real, and the wrinkled hand he held out, was not what reflected back to him.

Then to the right of his reflection, his father appeared.

He turned quickly to the shadowy room, only to find that no-one was there.

Slowly, one by one, more family members began to appear; some of which were from before his time. He began to wonder now if they had been waiting here since their deaths, awaiting the end of their bloodlines. And now that this had come to mind, he began to realize that others were here who had not been dead at the time of his accident.

Then his wife stepped from the crowd, and the thoughts vanished, along with his reflection. She was beautiful. They'd met when she was forty two, but she was no older than twenty now.

She reached out and touched the glass, and he returned the gesture.

As his hand made contact with the window, there was a feeling like rapid movement, and he found himself in the crowd.

Betty startled him by taking his hand.

Far off the sound of a train echoed out to them, and they walked out of the now well lighted lobby full of people, and into the bright sunlit day beyond to await a train which would take them to their final destination.

One he could only imagine.

THE FUTURE?

BY JOSEPH SWEET

Fiona stepped toward the front door, and then froze. The room took on a milky dreamlike glow, and goose bumps formed on her arms.

'I dreamed this, didn't I?'

The knock came again. Louder this time, and she found herself for the first time in months, unable to move forward.

Every time she thought of something to do to get herself out of this situation, the alternate path ran through her mind, and in all of them she died.

In a way she envied regular people. Those who could not see their futures.

Were she one of them, she'd have been dead years ago. People thought she was a genius, but a true genius didn't get a vision of the test score based on each choice they thought about making on tests. Or at least she didn't think they did.

In an instant, the idea to stand where she was and do nothing flew through her head, the thought being that maybe her would be assailant would leave, thinking that she wasn't yet at home.

The answer came just as quickly. He would gain entry by picking the lock, they would struggle, and she would get the gun away from him.

She waited.

Something slid into the lock. Clicked around.

The tumblers fell into place.

The door handle turned.

He came through the door with his weapon drawn.

She grabbed the gun and pulled him inward.

He gave a grunt in protest, but came sprawling forward nevertheless.

She was on top of him in an instant.

He began to struggle, and almost forced her off him, when she hit him with his own gun.

Minutes later he awoke, duct taped to a chair. His eyes rolled around in his head a couple times as he no doubt almost lost consciousness again, so she slapped him.

His eyes went wide with surprise, and then anger as he realized what had happened to him.

Only two alternates had passed before she found the right one this time.

"They'll know I didn't succeed and send someone else."

"So you're from the future?"

"How could you have known."

"There's only one flaw in your reasoning."

"And what's that?" The hate in his voice, was unbearable. For a second she was filled with it herself, before she managed to flush it out.

"If you hadn't succeeded they wouldn't have sent you to begin with. By just preparing to send you, they would have known whether or not you succeeded, because they are in the future. In fact in five alternate realities you did succeed. I just made you a part of one where you didn't."

"Impossible."

"Is it?"

"How?"

"I'm sure they made you study me. Made you get all there was to get on me, but the one thing your research would never tell you is that I am psychic. More than psychic in fact. I not only see what is going to happen, but every thought I have to stop what is happening changes the way things will occur, and in effect gives me a new vision, with an alternate outcome. You can't kill me."

"I will."

"Now. Tell me. Why would you *want* to kill me? Is it my theories on time travel? Theories, which no doubt will make what you've done possible."

"No!"

"Then what?"

"What you'll become will destroy the world."

She laughed then.

"What do you mean *what I will become*?"

"You are the anti-Christ."

She laughed then like she'd never laughed before.

"Okay, so you have a few screws loose, but what you fail to realize, is that you cannot stop me with time travel."

"Why?"

If you come back here to kill me, and you succeed, then you create a paradox, which could destroy the world anyway, only earlier. You see, if you traveled back in time to kill me, using technology that in this time I have not yet invented, you negate your purpose. A: If I died, I never did what it is you wish to kill me for, which means you never had a reason to go back in time, which means you never did, which means you never killed me. B: if I invent time travel, and I die before that happens, then you never had the means to travel back in time to begin with, which means you didn't, and none of this happens. Or C:, and this is where it gets fun. Both things happen, and since time cannot repair the events you've set in motion, it strives to put the wrong things right. And it can't because they all happened but didn't. And time itself is destroyed. In which case, you've managed to destroy the universe. And maybe not just one universe, but maybe many parallel ones as well."

"You're full of shit."

"Maybe, but I have to kill you now."

"Why?" he asked, fear evident in his voice for the first time since this encounter had begun.

"Because if I don't, you will kill me. I've seen three possible outcomes. One I let you go and you manage to get the drop on me. Two, I call the police and they come, but you get away and kill me in my sleep a few nights from now when you escape their custody. And the third one, is with me drugging you and leaving you in an alleyway but in that one, I am killed by some gang members. The high point to that one is that you are killed also. But then my responsibility to not letting that one happen is the whole universe destroyed one. The only feasible plan is shooting you and setting up the scene to look as though there was a struggle and I got the gun away from you but it didn't stop you, you kept coming, and backing me into a corner, struggling for the gun, my only chance was to kill you. And you know what?"

"I don't know, but I guess you're going to tell me."

"I won't spend more than a couple hours altogether talking to police, and they won't think about you twice. You'll just be some scum bag who broke into my apartment and tried to kill me."

"So you're just going to shoot me then?"

"You were going to shoot *me*, weren't you?"

"Yeah, but the problem is that I didn't."

"So I should just let you go so that you can keep trying until you succeed?"

"*There's* a problem with *your* logic?"

"And what's that?" she asked, knowing that he was just trying to buy time.

"If you were to let me go, I won't be able to kill you because you will always see an infinite number of possible outcomes until you see one which will allow you to survive."

"Yes, but who wants to take the chance?"

"Well another problem with your theory about the universe being destroyed if you are killed, is your belief of alternate universes, and the theories of alternate universes state that everything happens. Every possibility has occurred, which means that in some realities, I killed you, in others someone else did. In others you were mugged, in a car wreck, train wreck. Had a heart attack. Did develop time travel, didn't invent it. And if that is true, which you seem to think, then my killing you won't matter one bit to the universe, because somewhere else it still will happen. In which case, reality will shift and a balance will be created no matter what."

"Maybe you're right, but I don't believe you were ever successful in killing me in any reality. I just said that to intimidate you. I should have known they would send someone with brains. Someone who had done his homework. But, I'm afraid I cannot allow you to take up any more time."

"Why not? Is there a limit to when it's *safe to kill me*?"

"In a way. If I don't kill you in the next five minutes, Officer Riley won't be close enough to here in his patrol car to be the one who responds to the call and things may turn out differently. The next officer may question too much and my story may fall apart."

At that moment, Fiona realized that he didn't truly believe that he was going to die. Maybe that he thought she was just playing with his mind.

"So what is this guy's deal that makes him the one you need?"

"His mother was killed by a burglar, much in the way that I will tell this story."

"So ..." he began, but she cut him off.

"Sorry, times up." She aimed the handgun.

"No, wait." he said, perhaps taking her threat seriously for the first time.

She pulled the trigger.

SCAVENGERS

BY JOSEPH SWEET

*

Peter walked the cracked and pot-hole filled street slowly, lit only by the few remaining street lamps which still worked somehow, eyeing every shadow with suspicion and fear. His father had told him that the street lamps worked from solar energy, but either didn't know enough about it, or never felt the need to explain.

It had been five years since his father's death, and he had never made a supply run at night. But his food was gone, Rats had gotten in and eaten most of what he had built up, and contaminated the rest.

Row upon row of dead houses lined this street, and the next and so on. It seemed in fact as though the houses owned this town now, and he was an unwelcomed trespasser in this place which had once been home to his grandparents, and their ancestors.

His father had warned him never to travel at night. The scavengers would be out now, searching for food. And the cats.

Cats weren't the only small animal to change after the war. Many domesticated animals began to transform in the years to follow. Grow stronger. Evolve. Of course a great deal of it supposedly had to do with governmental research. Scientists had injected human D. N. A. into several types of animals in many different experiments over the years. Before the war, the research had reached a point where pigs could grow human parts, which could be used in transplants, cows also carried human genes. Cats were made bigger and stronger, but none of these animals were ever meant to be released into the wild.

And then there were the scavengers.

His father had told him that they were genetic creations from a government lab near here, or so it was rumored by the survivors. Part human, part animal. And some said, part alien. And now they were loose. Free to hunt whatever they liked.

This was a bad idea. In fact the more he thought about it, this could be the worse decision of his life.

Peter froze suddenly, certain that he was being watched. He was only able to keep himself from bolting by a dim hope that it was his imagination.

Then slowly, as he scanned the immediate area, they came into view.

Small yellow eyes.

They were everywhere.

Moving toward him.

As they closed in, he ran for the nearest building, stepping on one cat in the process and nearly falling to his doom right then, but perhaps by luck he managed to keep his balance.

Two lunged at him then, one of them managing to attach itself to his chest, one razor claw ripping across his face.

He cried out, and threw the dog-sized cat to the pavement, beginning to run again when more assaulted him.

He fell backwards, the air being knocked out of his lungs. There seemed no hope.

As they tore into him from all directions the loss of blood proved too great and he began to lose consciousness.

Somewhere above the darkness as he drifted off, there was a gunshot.

*

Peter awakened slowly to the smell of well seasoned meat cooking. For a moment he wondered if his father was still alive, and the last five years had all been a dream.

Then panic began to set in, as he realized how stupid that idea was.

He scanned the unfamiliar room, remembering the attack.

As he sat up in the bed he had never slept in before, he took notice for the first time of the bandages on his arm.

He pulled the blanket aside then and got out of bed, to find that his chest, stomach, and left leg had been bandaged as well, and that he was wearing boxer shorts that he had never seen.

He had not come across another survivor since he was twelve, and his father had left the camp they'd been in, to head back to this town.

According to him the rules were becoming a little more strict than he cared for; the colony was becoming too much like the old world had been before it.

He said that people should be learning from the past instead of trying to emulate it.

He had begged his father not to leave. He'd had friends there, but his father would hear none of it. He said they would be safer on their own. He said that the people running the camp had decided that no one would be allowed to carry weapons, except for the guards and people of importance. And he'd be dammed if he'd give up his protection with so much danger in the world now.

Peter hadn't fully understood, but he'd gone without much more of an argument.

Years later however, his father had returned to the camp; leaving him behind to protect the property, and their belongings.

When he returned he said that the place was in ruins. Everyone was dead.

It appeared that there had been no one left to bury anyone either. That or they'd simply fled in the heat of the battle and not returned.

Peter had obsessed over that for years. When his father was gone, who'd bury him when he died?

He'd never had the courage to go exploring on his own though. But now it seemed that someone had found him.

His fear turned to excitement. And what a hell of a time for them to come. Surely he would not have survived the attack, had it not been for the intervention of this person or persons.

He stood up slowly.

There was a candle on the stand next to the bed, which he picked up.

Carefully, he made his way toward the smell of cooking meat.

His stomach growled in anticipation of a meal.

As he reached the doorway to the kitchen, he froze.

What if this person was insane? What if he or she was a killer?

As he happened upon this last thought, he realized that none of it mattered, for the man was sitting in a chair not four feet away, watching him.

This would make escape difficult.

"I see you're awake."

"Yes." he answered, realizing instantly that he sounded afraid.

"I assure you, there is nothing to worry about. I do not intend to harm you."

'What an idiot I am,' he thought then. *'If he wanted to do anything, he'd have done it before.'*

"Sorry," he said finally. "Just new surroundings and all."

"And you haven't seen another person since your father died."

"How'd you ..."

"You talk in your sleep."

His hand shot out then, and for the first time, Peter tried to get a really good look at him. His pale fingers found a book of matches on the table and lit the cigarette which dangled from his lips.

The hood he wore concealed his features, and the sunglasses kept his eyes hidden as well.

"You're wondering why I wear sunglasses indoors, and cover my face."

"Well, yeah."

"I have a genetic disease. I can't be in the light, and my eyes are very sensitive."

“Oh.” he said simply, and he felt stupid for having nothing else to say.

“Are you hungry?”

“Very.” he admitted, his mouth watering.

The man motioned for him to take a seat, and put a few decent-sized pieces of meat on a plate, which had obviously been put out for him.

“Thank you.” he said, and began to eat.

After a few bites, he asked what he had wanted to ask before.

“Where did you come from?”

“Right here.” the man answered simply. “We’ve been here for years.”

“We?”

“Myself and my friends.”

“Really?” he asked, “I’ve never seen anyone around here.”

“Well we stay in most of the time during the day, and spend most of our time at the church.”

“Which one?” he asked, curious now as to how these people had gone all of this time unnoticed by either himself or his father.

“Why don’t I show you later?”

“Sure.” he answered, satisfied for the moment. “But I gotta know. What is this?” he asked, pointing toward the food.

“One of your attackers.” the man answered with a smile.

Peter suddenly felt as though he were going to be sick. But he repressed the urge to push the plate away, and even forced himself to take another bite. It was, after all, quite good, and who was he to argue with any kind of food in times like these?

In fact, he began to enjoy the thought of eating one of the bastards that had tried to kill him. After all, they had surely intended to eat *him*, hadn’t they?

After a few seconds though, he began to feel dizzy. He wondered for a moment if he’d lost too much blood, then he realized that the empty plate in front of his host was clean, He’d never eaten.

“You drugged me.” he tried to say, but it came out as, *“Yuh derg muh.”* which probably wouldn’t have made any sense to any but the person who said it.

He tried to get up, but fell to the floor with a thud which he heard but did not feel. He looked up as he began to lose consciousness and the man was standing over him, having removed the sunglasses and the hood. His hair was silvery and his eyes, the yellow reflective eyes of a cat.

Then there was darkness.

*

Peter awoke suddenly as though from a nightmare, remembering everything. He tried to move, but his arms and legs were bound.

He was in a church.

The stone altar beneath him wasn't cold, so he knew that he must have been laying like that for some time.

They closed in on him then. Several of them. They wore hooded robes, but they were down, exposing their faces.

There was a stinging and then a burning sensation in his arms as tubes with thick needles were inserted into the major arteries. Then another was inserted into an artery in each of his legs. Soon a transfusion had begun. They were taking his blood and giving him some of theirs.

This went on for hours, during which time, he could feel his body change, and after a short time had passed, he began to welcome it, and stopped fighting.

Then whispers at the back of his mind, which he just then began to notice, but he realized had been there the whole time, began to grow louder. He was beginning to hear their thoughts.

'You are one of us.' One stated, *'You will be so much stronger.'* another one assured him. *'Give in.'* another one said.

And then the tubes were ripped from his arms, and from theirs as well.

The wounds on his arms and legs healed almost instantaneously.

He was untied, and allowed to sit up then, the new strength flowing through his body, and he wondered if they had needed to untie him, or if he couldn't have merely ripped himself loose without much effort.

He wanted to break something - concrete perhaps - with his bare hands. Or rip something living apart; and was suddenly sickened by that idea, but at a far away part of his consciousness. He wondered vaguely how long that part of him would continue to protest if he gave in to those urges.

He looked around then at the tubing which lay on the ground in several places, blood having been spilled from them, and grieved for his lost life. His human life, for surely he was that no longer. He looked around the room, and saw that even the darkest shadows held no surprises for him.

He felt repulsed suddenly by the group and by himself. He was something he couldn't explain now, and these things around him had done it to him. He had been violated and unwillingly made a member of their species.

But another part of him felt great. Felt superhuman. Better than ever, and he knew that he would need to take action soon if he meant to do something about this, before he gave in completely to that other growing half.

Soon, he knew, he might smile while attacking other humans with this group. Perhaps even revel in it.

"You can do anything now." one of them said just then, seeming slightly unnerved by his thoughts, and he realized something.

They were all in a weakened state from what had just happened. He had been made stronger by their blood, but they had been made weaker by his.

"Yes." he said, stepping down from the altar, "I *can* do anything *can't I*?"

They began to back away then.

He moved so fast that it was a blur to his own eyes, but his movements were no less true to his will. Every blow struck exactly where it was intended, every slice of his claws tore through throats as he wished them to. In a minute or so, he'd torn through them all. Or so he'd thought.

After a few seconds of silence, standing there, covered in blood; he began to hear someone talking from another room, and a bolt slid into place.

Someone was behind the large double doors on the other side of the chapel. From the sound of it, they were locking themselves in.

His rage flared again, and he ran for the doors, slamming into them with as much speed and strength as he could muster, and the doors almost gave the first time.

On the second try, they busted inward.

He grinned as he saw the four of them, and wondered if these would be stronger since they had not been part of the process. But then he read from one of them, that when a person has been converted, for the first twenty four hours, he has the strength of ten. Ten men, or ten of these creatures; it didn't matter. He tore into them in a blur of movement, and it was over in seconds.

*

Hours later, he sat perched atop the stone cross at the top of the church, watching as the morning came. Soon the sun would be over the horizon and perhaps he would join his father, perhaps he wouldn't. They'd never said that the sunlight would kill them for certain. He only knew that one of them said he couldn't go out in it, and perhaps he had been lying to explain the need of sunglasses indoors.

Nevertheless, he would find out in a few minutes.

He watched the horizon as the sky changed from black to purple to blue, and waited. Prepared to accept his fate.

Whatever that may be.

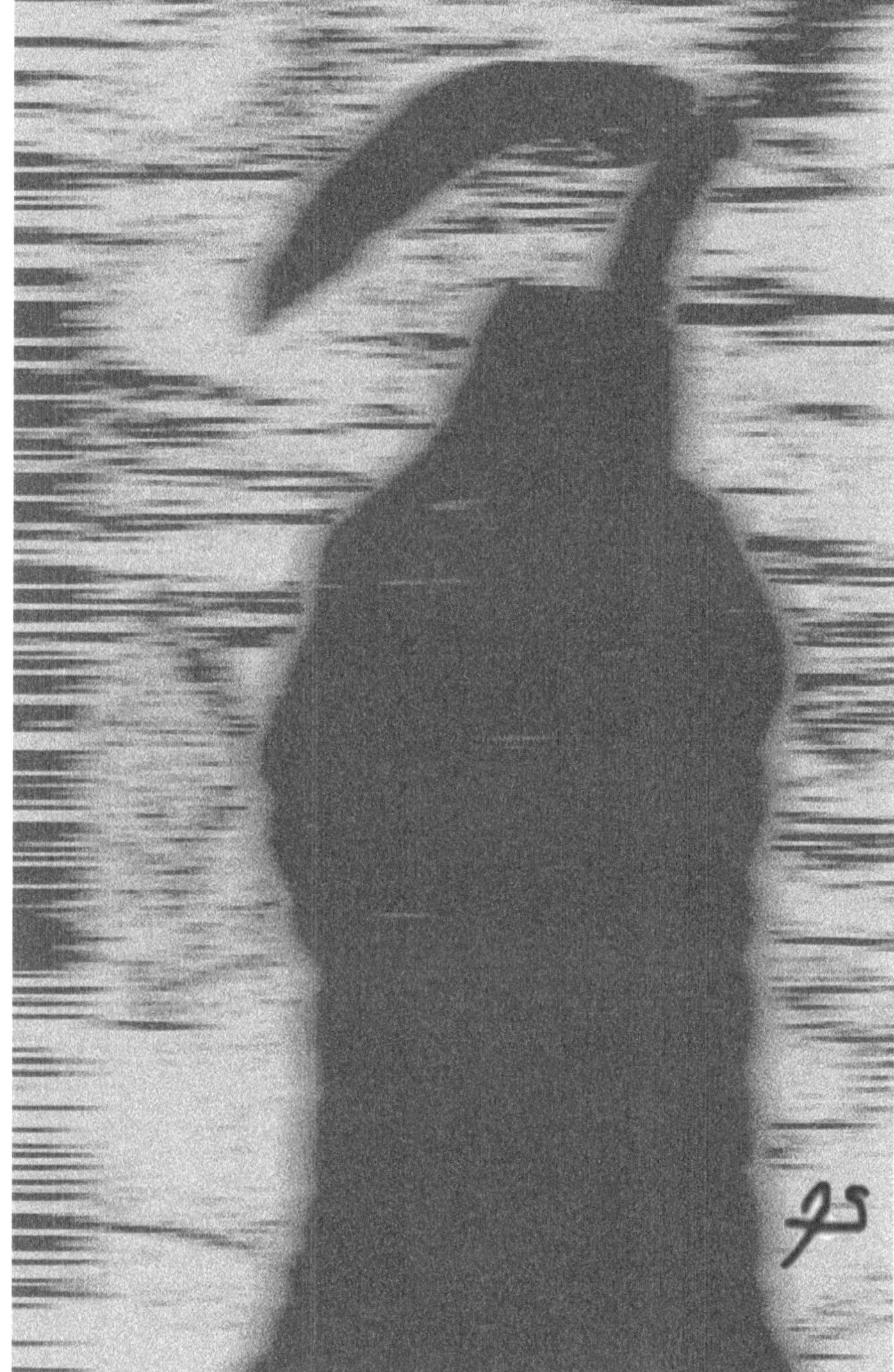

DEATH IN THE STORM

BY JOSEPH SWEET

*

In the distance, a town became visible through the sand.

The dust storm had kept him lost for what seemed days, though he had no recollection of setting out on this journey. He knew only that he'd gotten lost somewhere along the way.

His memories seemed buried in a haze which could surpass even the constant drone of sand, pelting him ceaselessly from all sides.

As he neared the first building, he removed the shirt which he'd been using to cover his mouth, and attempted to shield his eyes, but to no avail. The sand still made it through.

The first house had an enclosed porch.

He tried the door, but it was locked.

Not far away, music was playing.

Slowly he passed three houses. The visibility slightly better now with these new structures to guide him. Light was coming from a building not far away.

Through the blowing dust, he could nearly make it out.

Suddenly to the left there was movement.

He only barely heard it over the wind, but it had been there.

Just then, as he stopped he heard it again, and the darkened blur he only half glimpsed out of the corner of his eye, turned his blood to ice water.

He ran then with every bit of strength he had, toward the building, without knowing exactly what it was that had scared him. Something in that black shadowy blur had stirred a fear in him for which there was no explanation.

Whatever it had been, one thing was clear. He didn't want to see it up close.

He was pounding on the doors a moment later. The music stopped inside.

Footsteps neared the door, and a board was moved, unlocking it.

A man in a torn plaid shirt opened it, and eyed him suspiciously.

"Let me in." he pleaded.

The man looked him over, "Did you see its face?"

"No."

He stepped back reluctantly, seeming slightly relieved and let him in.

The group inside was not the sight he had hoped for. They seemed a depressed and partially insane bunch. All hope had abandoned them, or if any remained at all it could not be seen in their eyes.

The door was quickly locked behind him. As he watched the man slide the thick board into place, he wondered why they used such primitive methods, but at the same time, couldn't imagine what would have worked better.

He pushed the alien thought aside, and made his way to the bar, trying not to notice the looks on the faces of those here. Looks which seemed to pity him for finding his way to this place.

"Beer?" he asked, as he took a seat, pulling a small pouch from his side, which surprised him, as he couldn't recall ever having seen it before. He took a gold coin out and gazed at it curiously.

He had no idea where it had come from, but the whole situation was a mystery to him, so what was one more curiosity?

It was then that he noticed the woman behind the bar staring at the coin.

"You could buy a round for the whole bar with that." She stated.

"Well then," he said, amused at her comment, "You let me know if it runs out, and if I finish before that, keep the change."

As his hand fell to his side, it bumped across something there, and he was shocked to find an six shot revolver in a leather holster.

His hand remained on the butt of the gun for only the briefest of moments, but it was long enough that he could feel the tension in the room growing, so he returned his hand to the bar.

The bartender set his beer in front of him slowly, and asked, "You looking to cause trouble?"

"No Mam." he told her, "But I'd appreciate it if you could tell me where I am."

Her lower lip trembled for a second, and he swore she was going to cry, but she held her composure and said, "None of us know."

"What do you mean?" he asked, fear building in him once more.

"She means she doesn't know." a man said from behind him in a defensive tone that reeked of fear.

"How is that *possible*?" he asked.

"Do *you* know where *you* are?" the man asked.

"Well no." he answered.

"Then it's possible *aint it*?"

He grew silent then, trying to absorb it all. How could everyone not know where they were?

"I was confused too, at first," the woman said finally. "I stumbled across the bar. When I came there was no one here. I played the juke box to keep myself company. Then people started coming in, attracted to the sound of the music, I guess. A few from nearby houses. They'd found their way here just as I had. Then slowly more came. None of us know how we got here, or when the storm began.

"How can this be?" he asked.

"It just is mister." she answered.

"Well, how long can a storm like that last?"

"It's been years already." she grew distant for a second, then added, "Some of them think it will never stop."

"But how do you get supplies?"

"The basement is full of dry goods and kegs of beer. It all should last a couple more years."

"Has anyone tried to ..."

"Go out looking?" she finished for him.

"Well yeah."

"All who have, never came back. Some say the dark creature took them."

"The dark creature?" he asked, remembering the shadowy figure in the storm.

"We don't talk of him much. It makes people uneasy, but some were heard screaming the instant they disappeared into the storm. Those who went out after them were lost too, except for one."

"What'd he say?"

"He said a large creature made of shadows took them all."

He sat quietly then, unsure of what to say next. Wasn't that precisely what he had thought he'd glimpsed out there?

"What happened to him?" he finally asked.

"One morning, he just up and walked out into the storm."

He took a few seconds to absorb this. Something in it seemed important.

"Do you remember anything from before?" she asked him then, breaking his train of thought.

He tried as hard as he could to remember anything, but nothing came.

"No." he admitted finally. "*You?*"

She shook her head slowly.

She fished around then in a box off to the left, and looked at something, then moved her hand around again. As she did so, he could hear the clanking together of small metal objects.

A few seconds later she produced a key.

"What's this?" he asked.

"You'll need to sleep eventually. There are rooms upstairs. That one's empty." She blushed noticeably then, and turned away.

"I think I'll go now." he said, wanting to get away from the group. "Do I owe you anything for the room?"

"No, I still owe you change for the gold."

"Thanks." he said, and walked into the center of the room, looking around for a moment. He quickly noticed a corridor at the far end, and walked toward it.

Halfway down, he saw the stairs. Pleased with himself, that he had not needed to ask for directions, he continued on to find his room. Seconds later he was unlocking a door at the front end of the building on the second floor.

The room was dark, and unwelcoming in a way he didn't quite understand, but there was a lantern on the desk next to what would be his bed, and a book of matches.

The room filled with light with the lantern lit, but he almost wished he hadn't done it. The cob webs, covering almost everything except for the bed made the place seem older than time, and he felt as though he didn't belong here.

He looked out the window then, realizing that he most likely wouldn't be able to see anything. Slowly the visibility shifted and he could see a cloaked figure standing in the street outside. Its entire makeup seemed to shift with the wind, as though it wasn't much more than that, and then it was gone.

He wrote it off as sleep deprivation for the moment, and returning to the door, made sure it was locked. Then slowly he undressed, feeling as though he'd been walking for weeks. Every muscle was sore.

Just before he lay down, he placed the gun under his pillow.

*

Hours later, he awakened instantly in the darkness.

A key had been inserted into the lock on his door, and the handle was turning. Slowly it opened and closed, but the shadowy figure could not be made out clearly, as there wasn't sufficient light in the hallway.

The person slowly made their way to the bed.

His hand found the gun quickly, and quietly.

He waited.

The person was standing next to the bed now.

'Now or never.' he thought. He pulled the weapon out and aimed.

"Wait." a woman's voice said.

It was the bartender.

She placed her hand on the gun and pushed it down.

Her other hand pulled back the blankets.

"But."

"Ssshhh."

She slid under the covers and kissed his chest and neck, then mouth.

As she moved on top of him, the gun slid out of his hand, and to the floor.

They made love for hours, and fell asleep in the darkness, holding each other.

*

Early the next morning, he was awakened from his sleep by the sounds of a piano playing. Soft and sad, the music was, and it reminded him of something.

A funeral.

In an instant, it was as though he was there. As if the mere memory had transported him back there. A cold feeling sank into his stomach, and drifting upward; reverberated through his spine, causing him to shiver, but no-one took notice.

Slowly, he made his way toward the coffin. A woman was crying not far away, and he turned toward her, needing to see her. He wanted more than anything to see who was in this coffin, but somehow the crying was unbearable.

And he knew her, he realized as he neared her. "Christine?"

An instant later he was back in the room, the very meaning of the vision clinging to the edges of his mind, but falling fast.

He fought it, but in a few seconds it was gone.

The bartender was gone as well.

He decided suddenly to go back downstairs and find out who had been playing piano. He fumbled for a few seconds with the idea that she herself had just been a dream, but the smell of her was still on the sheets.

For a moment, he felt ashamed. As though he had committed some act of betrayal. But the feeling, and the smoke-like wisp of half forgotten memories it stirred, vanished just as quickly as it had presented itself.

Slowly he dressed. Still sore and feeling as though he hadn't gotten any rest at all, he made his way back down to the bar.

There weren't many people. Just two.

The bartender gave him a shy look, blushed and looked down.

The man at a table on the other side of the room, didn't look up at all.

"Was someone playing the piano a few minutes ago." he asked.

"No," she replied, looking a bit worried. "You heard the music?"

Without answering he walked to the piano in the center of the bar, and sat down. He ran his fingers lightly over the keys without pressing any of them, and slowly he remembered something.

A gathering of people. Their faces all concealed by the fog of unclear memory, but certainly this had been a sad event.

His fingers found a chord, and before he knew it he was playing a song.

The very song he had heard upon awakening, and slowly the event came back to him, for this music had been playing there.

"Christine?" he asked again, as he neared the woman who stood before the coffin, but she didn't reply. She merely continued sobbing, holding onto the edge of the casket for strength.

'How is it that I can remember her name, but I can't remember who she is to me, or even who I am?'

He reached out to comfort her by placing his hand on her shoulder, but his hand went right through her. And then his eyes were drawn to the one in the casket. The one he had wanted to see, but avoided thus far.

All the air seemed to disappear from his lungs, but had there been any air? Had he been in possession of lungs just then?

It was *he* who lay in the coffin. As he turned again to the woman he knew only as Christine, he realized who she was, and was ashamed that he'd been unable to remember. She was his wife, and the music that was simultaneously playing on the speakers here at the funeral and in the bar room from his fingers, was something he had written himself, although now he couldn't remember what it had been called. And now, as he neared the end of it, the vision began to fade, but it had faded then also, hadn't it?

Yes.

And then there had been sand.

A tear rolled down his cheek as he realized what must have happened.

He glanced around the bar now, and found that he had earned a fairly large crowd.

The bartender was standing beside him. He still didn't know her name he realized; but then again, the night before he would not have been able to give her his name either, so maybe she didn't know it herself.

"We've all heard the music playing at night, but none of us can play." She said, a look of bewilderment in her eyes, and perhaps hope.

"My name," he began, "is Jason Michaels." Everyone began stepping back at this point. Some of them afraid it seemed, although Jason couldn't imagine why.

The bartender seemed to be the only one unafraid. She took his left hand and stared at it, perhaps in awe of the music he'd just played, and then her eyes turned to his, and asked, "So you remember then?"

"Yes."

And then he felt the sudden urge to do something, and without even realizing that he'd done it until the act was over, he reached up and placed his right hand over her eyes, tightly gripping one of her wrists in his left.

She began to convulse under his hands for an instant and then went limp.

And he knew her name.

He only held her for a few seconds more before she came to.

"Do you remember anything now Sarah?" he asked her, and there were a few astonished gasps from the crowd.

"Yes," she answered, with tears spilling down her cheeks, then brought her free hand to the side of his face, "Oh, yes."

"So, is this hell?" he asked her.

"I don't think so," she replied, "but I think I know why the others left."

"They were ready."

Simultaneously, five of the group fled for the front door, and out into the sand storm.

There was a shadowy blur then from something and a figure standing there. Not clear enough to fully see, but there nonetheless.

Another woman from the group began walking, mesmerized toward the figure.

"No!" a man cried, and ran for her, just before she would have walked into the creatures embrace.

He was taken by it suddenly, and the woman walked to it just the same, and then the door slammed shut and the heavy board which served as a lock, put itself into place.

"You know what we have to do?"

"I'm not ready." Sarah replied.

"We'll both go when you are." he told her, and they began to head upstairs. There were only three people left in the bar.

One of them. The man who'd opened the door for him when he arrived, approached him, "Mister. Do for me, what you done for the lady?"

"I'm no different than you sir," he told him, "If you want to know, you will."

The man looked at him with fear and perhaps anger. "If that's true, then why were we here for two years before anyone woke up?"

"Are you sure that's true?" he asked him, and the man looked full of doubt, "From what I understand, several people just walked out into the storm, never to be heard from again. Maybe they had realized the truth."

"Or maybe that's why you're here." Sarah suggested.

Suddenly he was moved to try what he'd done to Sarah with this man, and he reached out again, barely conscious of the act until it was done, and covered the man's eyes with one hand and took one of his hands with the other.

The man. Zacherie, his name was, convulsed for a moment and went limp as Sarah had, then came to a few seconds later.

He smiled when he awakened, and went to the front door.

He turned back once, looking at the four of them, and then just walked out into the storm.

The two left came to Jason, and got on their knees.

"Stand up!" he barked at them, suddenly outraged without knowing why.

Maybe it was that they had actually bowed.

They looked at him with blank, frightened eyes. As though they thought he was going to strike them dead.

"I'm sorry," he apologized, "but you've no reason to bow to me."

He placed a hand on both of their foreheads, and in seconds they were gone into the storm.

"I guess it's just *us*." Sarah said after a few moments of silence.

"Do you think that's why we're here, you and me?"

"I don't know, but it couldn't hurt to wait a few days and see if anyone else comes."

"No, it couldn't" She replied, and they went up to their room.

*

Early the next morning, they awoke to sunlight, pouring through the window in their room, and Sarah got out of the bed, half believing what she was seeing.

Jason joined her at the window a few seconds later, bringing the blanket with him, and wrapped them in it.

She was smiling and crying at the same time, squinting at the bright light.

The storm had ended, and there were hundreds of people outside.

All of them wandering around, and some of them engaging in conversation, perhaps wondering where they were.

“Looks like we have our work cut out for us.” She said.

Jason and Sarah dressed as quickly as they could, and went downstairs.

He began playing the piano, as she unlocked the front door and wiped down the bar.

Slowly people began to filter in. Some seeking answers, and others merely drawn by the music.

JUST LIKE GOING TO SLEEP

BY JOSEPH SWEET

*

"Come on," the voice in the darkness begged with all of the urgency of a small child, whining to his mother for some candy. "It will be quick. Just like going to sleep."

She attempted to form words, but none came. Her dry throat produced nothing more than a rusty whisper, which could not be heard over the steady rumble of her stomach.

Laura wanted to scream out so badly that she could almost see the words forming in the air around her. Half of her wanted to say, "Yes, do it dammit. Just get it over with." but even if she chose to give in, she didn't think she could bring herself to let him win, even now.

When he spoke again, anger was evident in his voice. "Very well then." and that was it. The spotlight clicked off, and nothing but the ghostly purple trails which had been burned into her retinas remained.

Ironically she remembered the first line of genesis. *'In the beginning, there was nothing,'* and as she felt a smile fighting to surface, she wondered if the small bit of sanity which had remained with her this long had abandoned her, along with the rest of the world.

Laura absent-mindedly ran her fingers over the stubby protrusions that were her ribs, and wondered just how long she had been down here. Days? Weeks, perhaps? No not that long. Maybe one week at most, but she was sleeping more and more frequently now, and seemed despite the food deprivation, to be less and less hungry.

No doubt soon she would fall asleep and not wake up again.

The clanging of what sounded like a steel door slamming shut, echoed through the room, awakening her from deep thought. He was gone.

Why he seemed to need Laura's approval to kill her wasn't important. Although it made no sense. He obviously hadn't needed her permission to abduct her and bring her here. But since when did lunatics have to make sense? She'd be damned if she would give him the pleasure of hearing her beg for death.

As Laura once more drifted into unconsciousness, the man's words echoed in her mind. *"Just like going to sleep ... going to sleep ... sleep ..."*

"Please God," she prayed, "Don't let me wake up."

*

Laura awoke in her apartment, curled up on the love seat in her living room.

That had been one hell of a nightmare, seeming to have lasted over a week, but it felt now as if no time had passed at all.

She felt hungry all of the sudden. More so than she had felt in a long time, and she walked into the kitchen.

She opened the refrigerator, but it was empty. Confused, she opened the freezer door, but it also was empty.

Now near panic as her stomach growled; the room seemed to spin as a wave of light headedness fell over her, and she threw open the cupboards one by one, but they were all empty.

"Mommy?" her daughter called to her from the doorway.

She spun around quickly, almost losing her balance.

"Molly?"

Her daughter was standing in the doorway to the kitchen.

Then the man who'd abducted her, walked up behind her daughter and placed his hand on her shoulder. "Don't worry about *her* Laura. I'll make sure she's taken care of."

She snapped awake to the darkness of the basement once again. Wanting to scream, but not having the strength.

What if he went after Molly when he was done with her?

This thought was too much to bare.

*

He entered, slamming the steel door to make sure she awakened, but Laura had been awake for some time now.

She knew she would never allow herself to give in to his demand, and he wouldn't just let her go. As she'd lain there in the hours before he'd come back, a plan had formed. One she never would imagine in a million years would work, but she had to do something. And just maybe he'd put her out of her misery for trying.

She didn't flinch.

"Have you changed your mind yet?"

She remained silent, unmoving, restricting her breathing so as not to be heard.

"Hey, I asked you a question."

Laura's heart was beating so fast and so hard, that she was almost certain for a moment that he would hear it.

"I'm getting sick of you not talking," he said, "I don't have to *kill* you to make you sorry."

She almost gave in, in light of the threat, when she heard heavy footfalls on what sounded like metal steps. She tried to count them. Tried to create a mental picture as to what they must look like, and in which direction they would most certainly be.

One way or another it was too late to change her plans now.

Footsteps on cement now, growing ever closer. *'God, what am I doing?'* she wondered, frantically.

He was over her now.

"You *stupid bitch*!" he said, almost on the verge of tears, "*I* could have ended it *peacefully*. This must have been *hell* for you."

As confused as she now was, his crying made her want to scream in victory. Her animal side perhaps - she would think later - all that was left just then, responded to this weakness and brought the shackles which bound her hands together up and into his face, coming to her feet in the same instant.

Metal and flesh connected with a dull squishy thud, which knocked him off his feet.

Muscles groaned and stars danced around the corners of her vision, accented by a darkness which could have rivaled that of this room, but she managed to stay conscious. Despite the pain and waves of dizziness, she felt good.

Metal jingled nearby, and she quickly found herself scrambling for what she knew to be keys.

There was a sick moan and some sluggish movement a short ways off, as the son of a bitch no doubt attempted to unscramble his thoughts and figure out what in the fuck had just happened.

The world swam around Laura as she unlocked herself, and dropped the keys. Then she was running into the blinding white light, her body threatening to collapse every step of the way, but everything depended on her keeping moving.

There was movement behind her and something warm wrapped around her ankle, bringing her down on her face.

A flash of light, brighter than the one ahead, swarmed her as her head lightly connected with the cement floor.

In that instant, as she teetered on the edge of unconsciousness, she imagined that the darkness had formed hands to capture her, and would have most likely continued to believe it in her state, had the bastard not spoken.

"Bitch!"

"Nnnnnnoooo." she screamed, kicking desperately at the unseen man. Two of the kicks connected, and she was rewarded with a grunt from her would-be killer.

Laura used her moment of freedom to run toward the light again.

In an instant, she was past the spotlight, and could just barely make out the metal steps, ascending to a huge steel door.

In less than a second, it seemed, she reached the door, only to hear footsteps closing behind.

Laura slammed it behind her, and turned the first lock, then the second, and the third.

It only took her a second to realize that the door at the other end of this small passage was closed, and could be locked.

She turned to meet the killers' eyes, through a small square window in the door. He was dangling the keys, which she had so carelessly left behind.

Then he moved his hand down and unlocked the first lock. She could stand here and make sure he didn't unlock all three, but she didn't think she would remain conscious much longer in her current condition, so she turned and ran for the other door.

Surprisingly it wasn't locked.

She came out in a small living room.

It dawned on her then, that this man obviously would know his house better than she would, and any wrong turn could corner her. Then her eyes fell upon what she needed.

*

He burst through the door into the living room. His eyes, slitted in rage, widened almost instantly in terror as he noticed the gun in her hand.

Then cleverly the look vanished and he appeared calm. "I'm not going to kill you yet, but when I'm through, you'll be *begging* me to."

Ignoring his threat, Laura pulled back the hammer on the revolver, and he stopped advancing toward her.

He was still smiling though.

"Not loaded." he hissed.

"Oh yeah?" she asked and extended her arm toward him, applying the slightest bit of pressure to the trigger. It was so heavy in her hands, and she knew she was shaking, but she had the upper hand, nonetheless.

"Alright." he said, "You win." and he put his hands up, but there was something about that look on his face that said, he thought he could still get out of this.

"Oh, I see," she said, "You think, I'm going to call the *cops* and have them take you to *jail*."

"Well, otherwise it's *murder*."

"Self defense." she said, finding talking easier all the time.

"I have a wife," he said, in a calm voice, which was not the begging she had hoped for, but probably as close to it as she would get.

"Good, I'll be sure to leave her a note, telling her all about the things you did to me, and about all of the girls you told me about."

He lunged for her then, and perhaps it was luck, for surely her reflexes weren't that good, but she managed to shoot him in the stomach, and he fell sideways to the floor.

"Please." he began, creating a slight gurgling sound through the blood in his throat.

"Relax," she said, "It will be just like going to sleep."

With that, she aimed and put a bullet in his head.

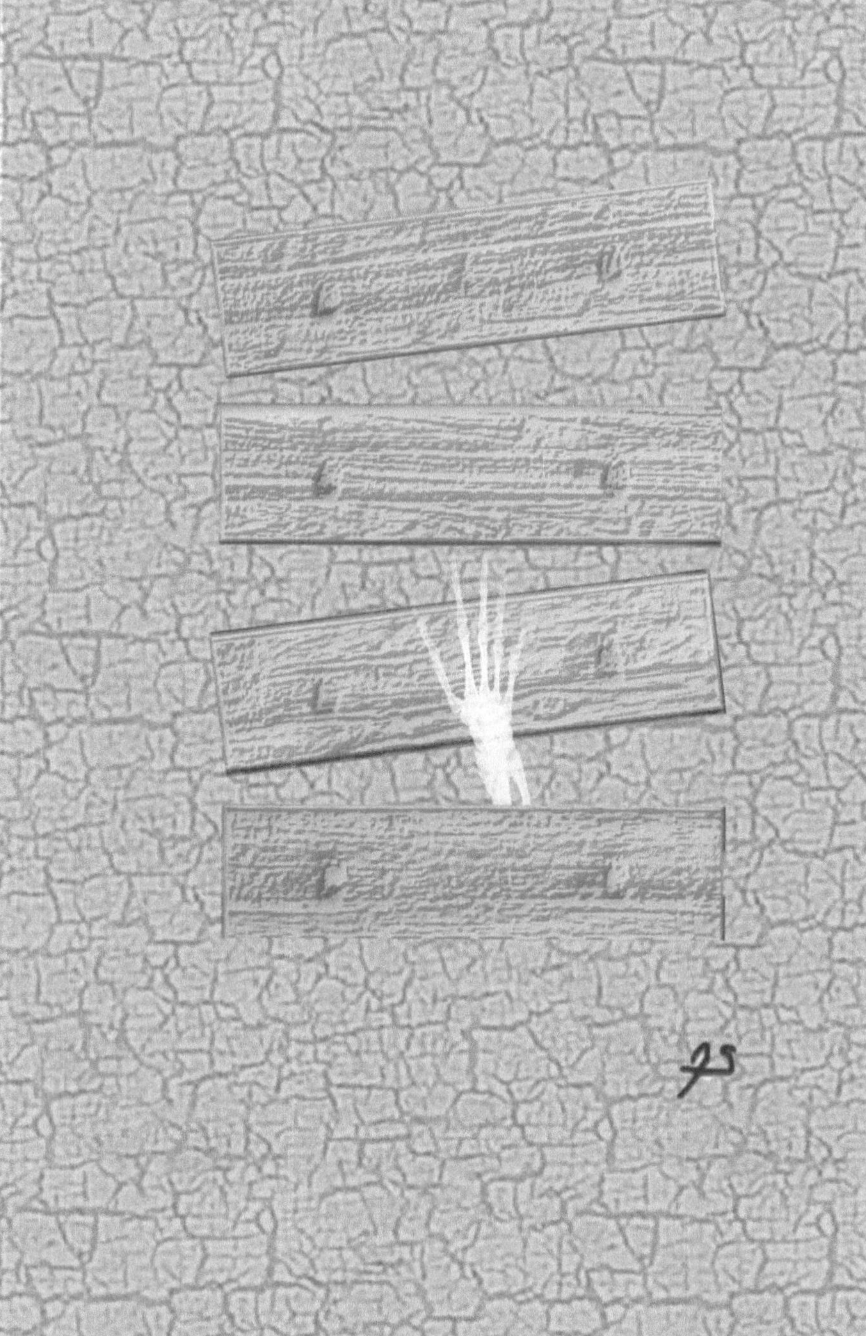

THE DRAWER

BY JOSEPH SWEET

*

Linda stared at the dresser for almost a full twenty minutes, trying to decide where it would look best in her room. It is a light pastel green walled room, with white drop-ceilings, and almost sherbet orange molding. She hates the room, but it will be painted to her liking soon, so that doesn't matter.

The dresser had been purchased earlier at a rummage sale.

While driving home from work she'd seen it there on the side of the road, and knew instantly that it would look great in her bedroom once all of the remodeling was finished. The neighbor boys had helped her get it inside and upstairs, but they were gone now.

She decided that it would look the best on the south wall, opposite the bed; and after a few minutes of grunting and pushing, she managed to get it to that position in the room.

She smiled once it was done. It was perfect. She knew that her husband wouldn't have cared where it went, and would probably give a satisfied grunt of approval no matter where she had put it, then turn away, bored, as though it were a foolish question. *'After all,'* he would probably think, *'it's just a dresser.'* Inside he would probably even be asking himself, *'What was wrong with the old one?'*

She probably wasn't giving him enough credit, but who cared. The point was that she liked it and he would have no valid reason to give her any trouble about it.

After about fifteen minutes, she managed to get clothes in most of the drawers, but was stopped abruptly when the bottom one would not open.

She wondered why she hadn't checked them all at the sale, but then again, the old man had seemed to be rushing her.

The drawer was jammed.

She quickly checked all of the other ones. They slid open and closed with ease.

Growing angry now, she dropped to her knees and pulled as hard as she could on the bottom drawer, but it wouldn't budge.

Well, it didn't matter.

She turned to leave the bedroom.

'But it did matter dammit.' She needed for some reason to know what was in that drawer.

She knew it was a bit odd to be obsessing so over it. After all, it was probably empty.

Linda forced herself to leave the room, and stop thinking about it. She went downstairs and poured herself a cup of coffee.

She went into the living room and tried to get interested in some sort of movie, but when none of the tapes or DVDs seemed to interest her, she realized that her mind was still on that damned drawer.

"Oh, *hell*." she said, and left the house. Before she knew what it was that she was doing, she found herself in the garage, searching through her husbands tools, looking for anything which would open that drawer.

She finally decided on a screwdriver.

She made her way slowly up the stairs, a smile slowly building. But she worked on the drawer until the screwdriver started to bend, and it still wouldn't open.

Finally she gave up. It was getting late anyway. After a while she convinced herself that her husband would be able to open it when he got home, and she started to get ready for bed.

She lay awake for an hour, before she finally gave up the natural route and took a valium. "Fuck you." she said to the drawer, thoughts of which had been what was keeping her up. She laid down, and after a little bit, sleep took her.

Sometime in the night, she awoke.

The re was a scratching sound across the room.

She turned on the light next to the bed, and after a few groggy seconds, realized with terrified certainty that the sound was coming from the dresser.

What had that old man done? She wondered, and she shivered at the possibilities.

She thought back to the sale.

The old man had stood there, looking at the dresser as though he didn't want to part with it, and part of her had thought it sentimentality or perhaps a show to make her want the dresser all the more, but another part of her had been on guard, afraid that it meant something else. Now, looking back it seemed that he might have actually been afraid of it. Or afraid to give it to her.

Had he perhaps put something alive in there, and then sealed it inside?

'Could be a cat,' she thought, *'Or a dog.'* She suddenly had to have that drawer open.

As she neared the drawer a few minutes later, with a hammer and another screw driver, the scratching stopped, as though in anticipation.

She stopped also, a fear creeping over her.

It knew she was there.

"Oh *stop it* you chicken," she told herself, "It's a *drawer*. What could actually fit in there, that could *hurt* you?"

But that was, she realized, a stupid question. Any number of small animals were capable of causing harm to a grown adult.

'Well,' she thought, *'There's only one way to find out.'* With that, she hammered the screwdriver into the crack at the top of the drawer, began to pry at it. Finally after a few seconds, there was an audible clicking sound, and the drawer began to slide, albeit very slowly. It was like trying to open a door with hinges that were completely rusted.

And then it pulled out all of the way.

And it wasn't a cat, or a dog, or a mouse, or any other manner of small animal; it was a human body.

Its bones had been rudely broken and the body folded in order to be fit into the drawer, but otherwise was in one piece.

Linda backed away slowly, trying to fight the scream which was building inside her.

And then one of its eyes opened, and she lost it. The screaming droned away until she thought that she'd lost her voice, and then she realized that she was in fact still screaming, it just sounded far away.

Something hit her from behind, and she suddenly realized that she had backed into a corner.

The man in her drawer was twisting his body this way and that with a lot of cracks and tearing sounds, and soon, she could see, he would be in a fully upright position.

She realized her mistake then.

She had backed away, not caring where, as long as she got away from the abomination in her drawer, and had moved quite a ways from the bedroom door, which was probably her only avenue of escape. Now the thing was between her and her exit.

She began to stand, and slowly to move toward it.

The thing's head swiveled toward her, and then fell to one side of its misshapen shoulders, with a thick liquid crackle, before being righted by the left hand of this monster that looked human. With a couple of snaps and cracks the head was in its proper position, but since turning toward her, its eyes had never left hers.

Its mouth opened, but no sound came out. Its jaw hung at the wrong angle, but quickly snapped back into place.

She knew what it wanted though, regardless of the lack of sound.

It wanted her to take its place.

"NO!" she screamed at it, and ran toward the door.

Its hands reached out lightning quick, still crackling, but almost whole again, and latched onto her shoulders.

She tried to get away, but it was pulling her toward it.

She saw her chance and went for it a second later.

The screwdriver had been dropped on the floor when the drawer had come open all of the way.

She stooped down and grabbed hold of it, before being yanked back up to face the monster.

In one swift move, she lifted the screwdriver into the air, and stabbed it in the eye.

Linda cried out then in pain like she had never known.

She had stabbed *its* eye, but *hers* was bleeding.

"Oh God," she cried.

It had let go of her now.

She reached up and tried to take hold of the screw driver which was now in her right eye, though luckily not all of the way, but she couldn't do it. There was too much pain. And then she lost consciousness.

*

Mark arrived six hours later, having left the conference early when he hadn't heard from his wife in three days.

On occasion, she had forgotten to take her medication, and her depression had grown until she tried to hurt herself.

He called out for her when he got inside.

The kitchen lights were on, and there were dishes in the sink, but they had obviously been there for days, as a scum had started to build up on them from the water they had been placed in.

He rounded the corner toward the stairs, calling her name more urgently.

"Linda?" he called, running up the stair now, as he could see from the bottom that the bedroom light was on.

At first glance the bedroom was empty, and then he saw what he had at first mistaken for dirt or clothing on the floor out of the corner of his eye, for what it actually was. Pools of blood. The biggest of which was centered around their dresser, which he would have noticed as new, had it not been for all that blood. He only half noticed the dressers new position from their old one.

Slowly he walked toward it, being careful not to step in any of it, his heart beating a mile a minute, terror building in him with each step as to what he was going to see.

On the floor a short distance away was a hammer, and it looked as though someone had broken into the bottom drawer of the dresser. It was now that he realized this was not the same one as had been here before.

All around the top of the drawer were scrapes and missing chips of wood, where it looked as though a screw driver had been used. There was a scraping sound from within.

He was standing in the blood now, needing to see what was inside that drawer.

He dropped to his knees. Grabbed the handles. Pulled it open. And he cried out in terror.

His wife had somehow managed to fit herself into the drawer, breaking a couple limbs in the process. There, jutting out from where her right eye had been, was the screw driver she had used to open it.

"Jesus." he breathed. Reaching a hand out to touch the side of her face, which proved to be cold and clammy, and he wished he had canceled his trip the first time he hadn't gotten an answer when he'd tried to call her.

"I'm sorry babe." he said.

As he spoke the words, her left eye opened and turned to look at him.

Mark cried out, backing slowly from the dresser, unmindful of the blood he was smearing all over himself and the floor.

'Can't be real.' he thought. There was no way she could be alive. Not like that.

Mark watched in terror as she began to rise up, snapping bones back together one by one, never taking her eyes off him.

At some point, shortly after realizing that he had wet himself, he lost consciousness.

CRASH LANDING

BY JOSEPH SWEET

Grace and Eddy were both beat, and they knew it. The trip had nearly sucked the life out of the two of them.

They'd just passed an exit to a town called Watertown, and Grace had been tempted as hell to ask her husband to stop and find a hotel.

Eddy thought of asking her to switch with him for driving, but knew that she'd likely last no longer than he would. The thought of a hotel had crossed his mind once or twice, but what kind of name was Watertown? In his mind he saw farmers with pitchforks, spittin' tobacco, and staring at their sisters in a way that wasn't good in front of a sign which listed a population of twelve.

Up ahead a truck stop became visible.

"You want some coffee?"

"Huh?" Grace mumbled, having been almost asleep.

"Coffee?" he asked again, pointing toward the truck stop.

"Oh." she started, "Yes. You want me to drive for a bit?"

"No that's okay." he replied, "You're tired too. I just need a little caffeine."

With this they pulled in and parked between two large trucks.

"I'll get it." she said, wanting to get some fresh air.

"Okay." Eddy answered, shutting off the engine, and preparing to get out as well. Having been driving for fifteen hours, the last place he felt like being was in that car.

As she headed for the little twenty four hour shop, he made his way to a bench. Taking a deep breath of the cool night air, he sat down prepared to relax for the hour it would most likely take her, talking to the cashier, and deciding on which flavor of coffee she wanted.

He closed his eyes.

Just then two men broke through the bushes, less than twenty yards away.

Eddy looked up to see these newcomers.

They were both in suits.

The first one began towards him, pulling a gun as he closed the distance.

Eddy froze, never having had a gun pointed at him before.

“Where’s your car?” the man demanded to know.

He took out his keys, prepared to hand them over. The shit box he drove, not being worth his life.

“You’re driving,” the man said, “now get up.”

The other one pulled a weapon now.

Just then another man appeared from the row of large pine trees behind them.

The first one, a tall black man of about thirty or thirty five, turned back to this one, aiming the weapon at him now.

The other kept his aim on Eddy.

“Get to the car.”

Eddy was about to go with them, not wanting to involve his wife in this, when she came out earlier than he had expected.

She got halfway to him before she realized what was going on.

“Eddy?” she called, uncertain, “Everything okay?”

‘No,’ he wanted to say, *‘I have a gun pointed at my head, how do you fucking think things are?’* but he only looked in her direction, and said, “Go back in the store.”

“That yer wife?” the second man asked. This one a rather pale individual, a snide grin oozing across his face which said, *‘Not bad buddy, not bad at all.’*

“Don’t think about it honey.” he said to her when Eddy hadn’t answered, “Get over here, or I shoot your hubby.”

“Stop!” the first one yelled at the newcomer, who was still advancing toward them; but this one didn’t seem to care that he had a gun pointed at him, and just kept walking.

"Get in the car!" he commanded again.

This time Eddy did as he was told, going to the driver's side of the vehicle.

Grace was about to get in the passenger side, when the black man took her hand and said, "Not what I had in mind."

Eddy began to panic as she was seated in the back with the other guy, who just seemed to stare her up and down, his eyes coming to rest finally on her tits.

The third man was closing in then.

The black man, raised his handgun. Aimed.

The newcomer, pale and pimply faced, but in a suit like the other two, began to change then. His eyes began to glow green, his face starting to transform. It screamed at them. A high pitched inhuman screech, which caused the hair on the back of Eddy's neck to stand up, and his heart to beat wildly in his chest.

The man fired twice, hitting the creature in the forehead with both shots.

It caught fire and exploded, as he sat in the passenger's seat and closed the door. "Let's get going." he said.

"Where are we headed?" Eddy asked then.

"Just get back on the highway and drive for now."

He did as he was told, glancing in the rear view mirror every few seconds to keep an eye on the other one, who now had a hand behind Grace, and was still staring.

She looked away, ignoring him the best she could.

"Okay." the man in the passenger's seat said finally. "I'm going to put this away." He put his gun back in its holster then. "I just needed to get you two moving back there."

"What was happening to that man's face?" Grace asked suddenly.

"He was an alien." the man stated simply, as though this were the most common thing in the world.

"What?" asked Eddy, disbelieving what he'd just heard. *'Yah,'* he thought, *'he was an alien, and I'm the incredible fucking hulk.'* he thought for a moment, then tried to imagine himself in green makeup, roaring and throwing cars, and almost broke into laughter.

"An extra terrestrial life form." the man in the passenger seat continued, then paused, taking a deep breath. "At least, that's what he was changing into."

"I don't understand." Grace stated.

"My name's Hugo." The man said to her, reaching into the back seat to shake her hand. "I work for the government; although alien's wasn't my specialty."

"Victor." the man beside her added, putting out his hand as well.

Grace looked at him for an instant only, then turned back to Hugo without taking his hand.

"So what the hell happened back there?" asked Eddy, growing slightly impatient with this whole ordeal.

"Alright." Hugo started, "We were all headed toward Canada, from where we were staying in Watertown. I'm sure you saw the turn off not too far back there."

"Yah." Eddy stated, remembering having seen the sign, having wondered what the hell kind of name it was for a town. It was like naming a place, Grass-town, or sky-town.. or even earth or air-town. It just sounded ridiculous.

"Well, as you can see, we didn't get very far. There were some very odd lights in the sky. All of them following along beside each other. We pulled over, thinking that we were probably imagining it. Or that they were a bunch of helicopters from Fort Drum. But there was no sound.

As we got out of the car, one of the lights broke free from the rest, as though it had lost control. We watched as it crashed down not a half a mile into the woods from where we were standing. Frank was the first to say that we should go check it out."

"The guy you shot?" asked Eddy.

"Well, yes." Hugo replied, "Minutes later, we found the ship, and it appeared to be a flying saucer. There were markings all along the sides. Strange, almost like hieroglyphs of some kind. I turned to Frank, but he was gone. Me and Victor looked for him for almost twenty minutes. Then it came at us.

We were separated. We both started firing at it, but it took Victor down.

I shot it in the head once, and it fell to the ground. A neon blue looking substance - I guess it was the thing's blood - was kind of oozing out of the hole I'd made. Victor got to his feet, and we rounded the craft. On the far side, there was an opening. Smoke was pouring from it.

I crawled inside, pulling a small flashlight from my pocket. There were dead aliens all over the inside. It seemed like there was more of them than there was room for.

Then in the center, what looked like a small nuclear reactor, and a readout on a small monitor. I couldn't read it of course, but it was obvious to me that something bad was about to happen. Looked like it was about to melt down or something.

I crawled back out, and told Victor we needed to get as far from there as was possible."

"That's when you found us?" Grace asked.

"Yup." Victor said, from beside her.

"Only a couple minutes later." Hugo added.

"Of course, you left out the part about Frank." Victor reminded him.

Hugo shot him a glance which said, *'there's something wrong with you'*, having wanted to forget that part, but he continued on. "Well, we were almost to the truck stop, having become disoriented. We had no idea which way the car was. And as we were about to reach the place, Frank called out from behind us."

"He tried to bull shit us at first. Make us think he'd passed out, or fallen down." Victor added.

"I don't know," Hugo started again, "If he was actually able to recall what had happened. He started walking toward us, and his eyes started to glow. I immediately pulled my handgun. He screeched at us, just as he did in front of you two."

"Why didn't you shoot him then?" asked Eddy.

Hugo just looked at him for a minute, then answered. "Because he'd been our friend. We hung out, drank beer, and played cards with this man. He'd been there with us for years. It's not easy to just up and shoot someone you've known that long."

"Sorry."

"It's okay." Hugo stated, then fell silent, his eyes locked on Victor in the back seat. "What are you doing?"

Eddy turned his attention to the backseat so quickly that he almost drove off the road.

Victor was aiming his gun at Hugo, grinning. His eyes were now beginning to pick up some of the glow.

"I can hear them now." he said.

"Put down the gun." Hugo demanded.

Eddy eyed the dark road ahead and noticed a turn off, taking it as quickly as he could, only to find himself on an empty road. Then, just visible up ahead, was a house.

Thinking quickly, he reached to his side, flipped the switch, first locking the back passenger side door, then unlocking it, to get Grace's attention.

She looked into his eyes in the mirror, and seemed to understand.

Pulling into the driveway, he realized his mistake however, as the house appeared to be abandoned.

Victor's eyes were nearly illuminating the whole inside of the car now, and his facial features began to change.

"Make it stop." he cried.

"We will," Hugo said softly, "just give me the gun."

Victor aimed it at him then, only inches from the man's face. Then seemingly without thought, pulled the trigger.

Grace was out of the car, running, but as Eddy attempted to do the same, Victor pointed the gun at him, and fired.

Eddy dove out of the car, just in time to keep from getting killed.

He searched all over for Grace, then noticed that the house didn't have a front door. He ran for the entrance then.

Behind him, the creature gave out a hellish shriek.

He looked back as he reached the door, to see it standing there. The face almost human still, but the rest of the body was definitely alien. The man's nose had begun to sink in and his eyes were very much like cat's eyes, and glowing green. It pointed at him, and as it did, tiny quills jettisoned from its arm.

One of them hit him in the neck, another in the shoulder.

He fell backward, a strange rush of energy pulsing through him.

"Oh God." he said, certain he knew what was happening. He almost didn't even notice the thing leap over him on its way into the house.

Voices began to invade his thoughts then, and he forced himself to his feet.

Making it slowly to the car, he opened the passenger side door.

Hugo fell out onto the gravel driveway.

A sudden sharp pain in his head hit him so badly that he fell to the ground. The voices were slowly becoming understandable now.

They wanted him to become. To protect the mother. By this they meant earth. The planet they were about to take over. He reached over slowly, his body almost not under his own will, and found Hugo's gun. In the house, he heard Grace scream. He knew he could go to her. Try and save her, perhaps. But then he might also change and end up killing her himself. "Forgive me honey." he said bringing the weapon to the side of his head.

Darkness fell as he pulled the trigger, and he knew no more.

Three seconds later the reactor in the alien ship went critical, and exploded, destroying them and everything else for miles.

DEADLY MEMORY

BY JOSEPH SWEET

I

Brian awoke in a cold sweat. A bright flash in the night ... The smell of sulfur. Someone had been shot, but who? In a few short seconds, the answers to his very existence had flashed before his eyes, then vanished just as quickly.

The electric door to his room slid open then, and Victor walked in, a smug look on his face as usual.

It was as though the man thought Brian owed his life to him.

"Bad dream?" he asked.

"Yah," he replied, noticing the nervous raising of Victor's eyebrows, "I dreamed you and me were related."

"Funny." He stated in a dry sarcastic tone, although it was obvious from the look on his face that he wanted to backhand him.

"*I* thought so." Brian mumbled under his breath, shrugging, and wondered what he had ever done to make this man hate him so.

"So, what did you *really* have a nightmare about?"

"Dreamed I'd been shot."

"Hmm."

"So what's it mean?"

"Doesn't matter." he stated with a fake smile, "It was just a dream, right?"

"Well then, why the hell did you ask?"

"Watch your mouth."

"Hmm, I can't remember the last time I was *so sorry.*"

"Kill the sarcasm, you'll be meeting your mate today."

"What if I don't like her?"

"The computer says you will."

"Who gives a *shit* what a *computer* says?" Brian asked, outraged that a machine had decided his fate for him.

Mary walked in at that moment, pushing a tray with his breakfast on it. A disapproving look on her face.

"Sorry Mary." he said.

"You'd better curb that language, or I'll take your breakfast back."

"That'd be cruelty to animals." Victor replied with a grin.

"Oh get the hell out of here you prick." Mary shouted, swatting at him with a rolled up paper.

He ducked her swing, and walked out of the room, laughing his little troll laugh. Brian swore the man was evil in some way.

"*My* language?" Brian scolded her, then smiled.

"Aint much of a roll model am I?" she said.

"You're the best."

She sat on the side of his bed then, a serious look passing over her. She actually seemed to care so much for him. And she was the closest thing to a mother he'd had.

He wanted in that instant to hug her and cry, but he was too old for that.

"You still havin' those dreams?"

A cold chill moved slowly up his spine.

"Yeah."

"Don't you go telling him, or anyone else about 'em, you hear me?"

"Yes."

"I didn't say this, and you just remember that. But if you tell them, you'll be in danger. Don't you forget it."

"But, why?"

"Just trust me."

If he'd known his mother, he'd have imagined her to be like Mary. She seemed to genuinely care about him. There was a fear just below the surface of her smile however, which scared him. She knew something horrible. Some truth she didn't dare admit, even to herself. She'd never tell him what it was, and he was pretty sure that if he did know, he wouldn't live long enough to tell anyone else about it.

At times he figured that he was just paranoid. But if he'd known how real that danger was, maybe he'd have run sooner.

There were dreams he hadn't told Victor about. Dreams so bizarre he tried not to think about them, and they were coming more frequently now.

"So why do *you* hate him so much?" he asked, mainly to change the subject of his thoughts. "I mean, other than the fact that he's a jerk."

She gave him the strangest look then. "He's a *bad man*. You remember that. And that's all you need to know."

II

George stepped out onto the street. This was one of the last cities.

As impossible as it would seem, he remembered how it was here six hundred years before the war. He remembered it as though he were there yesterday, because in his memories, he had been.

They were watching him. He was being considered for code red clearance, and for that they needed to trust him completely.

If they knew the memories he had, more of which were surfacing each day, or of the dreams each night of a time and place in which he could not have been, he'd be dead.

He knew it somehow. Because it was more than just past life memories.

He was not a natural part of this time, and he knew this with a growing certainty. As strange as the thought seemed, he'd been brought here from his true time. There was no way to explain it yet.

But when he had clearance, he'd figure it out. With access to the database, and top clearance for the current project, he'd find out what was going on.

And then there was Brian. He was a key to figuring this out as well. Not only because he was part of the memories, but because the two of them were a part of the council's plans.

*

"George." Frank shouted from across the courtyard. George turned to see him waving his hands by the entrance.

He picked up his pace. "Hey," he said, trying not to sound nervous. "What's up?"

"Krieger sent me out here to give you your new card."

"Already?"

"Yup." With that Frank handed him a red plastic card with a hologram of his face, and a magnetic strip.

"Well that was easy." he said, "I thought they'd make me take a few hundred tests or something."

"Apparently not. Now *I* on the other hand, had to take at least a *dozen tests*, and *two years* of classes. But then again, I'm not a clone."

"I was going to ask, but I was kind of afraid to. Just who am I a clone of?"

"Ah ah Georgy, them's the kind of questions'll get that card taken back."

"What would it hurt for me to know who the blood donor was?"

"Well I guess it wouldn't, but you be sure you don't let any of the kids know they were cloned."

"Yeah I remember, but what's the difference between them and me?"

"You mean why did we tell you that you were a clone, and not them?"

"Exactly."

"Because your aging was accelerated and theirs wasn't."

"So you're saying that it's easier for an adult to accept such a thing, than for a child. Even if they were born at the same time?"

"Listen, George. I'm only going to say this once. Questioning the council isn't the best thing to do. They're paranoid. And if they think for an instant that they can't trust you, your life would be in danger. After the first group of clones, you can't blame them."

"I thought we *were* the first batch. What are you *talking about*?" he asked, concern obvious in his voice.

"I thought you *knew*." A mixed look of embarrassment and fear passed over him. His eyes darted back and forth across the street, and he quickly scanned the surrounding area to make sure no one was close enough to hear what he was about to say.

"No."

"*Jesus.*" The look was panic now.

"*What?*"

"I guess I *have* to tell you now. But if you tell *anyone*, they could make me disappear."

"I won't tell a soul."

"Okay. The first clones remembered the lives of the blood donors."

"And that's catastrophic *why*?"

"You don't understand. They were starting to remember *both lives*. This one, and the life of the person who was cloned. With each day the memories of the past life became more and more vivid, until the two realities were too much for them to handle and they went insane."

"What did they do with them?"

"They were terminated."

"I hope you mean pink slips."

"No I mean gassed."

"Jesus. Well how did they fix the problem this time?"

Frank just looked at him. "I don't know." There was a look of fear so strong, George wanted to hug him, but figured he wouldn't exactly take it the right way.

"And," he added, "I don't ask!"

III

Brian stepped into the huge plastic cylinder for his daily testing.

"That's it," Victor said, the grin on his face making him more and more nervous by the minute.

Suddenly he was in a much bigger room, with a lot more kids. He looked around at them in a daze. All of them looked scared.

The room was filled suddenly with a hissing sound.

Everyone began choking, including him.

He could feel consciousness slipping away, as he fought frantically to find air which simply wasn't there anymore.

Suddenly he was back in the small tank. He'd fallen to his knees without knowing it.

Victor was already standing in front of the cylinder, waiting for it to open. He was holding a gun.

"What's *that* for?" Brian asked, as the tube opened.

"What happened?"

"I don't know," he lied, "Everything, just went white."

For the next hour, he sat in the same room. Twice the tests had been done on him than had been scheduled. *'What,'* he wondered, *'would it hurt to tell them what I saw?'* He was about ready to say whatever they wanted to hear if they would just let him out of here.

Across the room, Victor was arguing with a man Brian had never seen before. His words were just loud enough for Brian to catch something he didn't like.

"It's happening again."

"Stay calm," said the other man, "In the last one, it happened at least two months before this."

"He knows."

"The donor had seizures. And based on the original documents we had on him, they didn't always show in tests."

"This wasn't a *seizure.*"

"That is *your* opinion mister Caldwell, and I *do* suggest that you keep it to yourself. Now go tend to the boy."

Brian closed his eyes so they would think he'd fallen asleep on the table.

He could feel victor watching him from only a few feet away.

"Hey, shit head."

Brian opened his eyes, and looked around, doing a pretty convincing job of acting as though he'd just been awakened.

"The doctors say you're okay, so get dressed and get outta here, and make sure you're ready after dinner."

Brian frowned at this. He knew what it was that he needed to be ready for, and he wasn't all that interested.

They were going to introduce him to his mate.

There was no reason to talk about it. They were going to make him do it, and he knew that he had no say in the matter.

"Oh yah." Victor added, as he neared the door.

"What?"

"Your *fag* buddy is here too."

"George?" he asked, ignoring the insult toward his friend.

"Yah. Just make sure you're back in time for dinner."

IV

George looked to be in an especially good mood today.

"Hay there Bry," he started, "Wanna get outta this place for a while?"

"Hell yah."

A few minutes later they were driving.

"So, where're we goin?"

"Sackets Harbor."

"Really?"

"Yup."

"Why there?"

"Well, I figured it would be quiet, and we could just hang out. Maybe go fishing."

"Wow."

"I brought dinner too."

"Victor said I'd have to be back by dinner time."

"Well Victor probably didn't know that I got permission from higher up to let you have dinner out there with me."

George reached into his jacket and pulled out a small device with a wand on the end, and began to hold it out over Brian's chest.

"What are you doing?"

"Tell you in a minute."

He moved it down toward his shoes, and back up over his body again.

With a satisfied grin, he put the device back in his pocket.

"What was that?"

"I was just making sure you didn't have a bug on you."

"A *bug*?"

"A *listening* device."

"Who would be *listening*?"

"Someone who didn't want me to tell you the truth."

"About what?"

"Those dreams you've been having."

Brian could think of nothing to say. He half wanted to tell him all about them, but Mary's words were still haunting him, so he kept quiet.

"You'll understand when we get out to Sackets."

They drove in silence after that.

V

They drove through the empty little town quietly, all the while chills moving through Brian's body; he knew this place, and it wasn't just a feeling of having visited once before, but one of having lived and grown to adult-hood here.

The knowledge that he was only seventeen, did enter his mind, but he had been tempted to find a mirror a couple times. Just when he thought he was going to ask George to turn around and take him back, they pulled onto main street.

He was silenced then by the utter desolation of the place. It was as though he'd been here earlier today and the place had gone to hell in only a few hours.

Then they were stopping.

"Do you remember this place?"

"Oh my God."

He was stepping out of the car without fully realizing it.

They had come here together as friends, to eat and enjoy the summer day.

"I've wanted to come back here for a couple years now." George stated.

"We had fun that day."

"So you remember?"

"How?"

"Well you were about ten years older. And I was a few years older myself, but we were here about six hundred years ago."

"Was it a past life?"

"Now you see, *that's* an interesting question. I know for a fact that none of your classes, or anything they've exposed you to, has had anything to do with reincarnation... Yet you know what it is."

"Because I knew then."

"*Precisely*, but it isn't reincarnation."

"What then?"

"It's better if we go inside." With that he walked around the car to the back passenger seat and retrieved their lunch.

Once inside, in near complete darkness, George fished out a flash-light and made his way to a fuse box. A few seconds later, they had electricity. "Before you ask, I wired this place up weeks ago."

"Nice."

They headed down the long ramp, toward where he knew the bar would be, and George cautiously pushed open a door that had once been made almost entirely of glass.

Off to the left, he could just make out the kitchen through a doorless walkway, as they rounded the corner, and turned right onto the dock.

Sitting there, overlooking the water, where George had setup a table for them, the conversation continued.

"So," began Brian, "what is it?"

"What?"

"You said it wasn't reincarnation, so what is it?"

"Cloning."

"You're kidding."

"Nope."

"So who am *I* a clone of?"

VI

While Brian and George were driving to Sackets Harbor, Victor was talking to the head of the council, Francis Meadows.

"Look, I'm not questioning your judgment, but I don't think it was a good idea."

"What could it hurt to let them have a nice quiet day?"

"That's where he grew up, that's what it could hurt."

"Exactly."

"Okay, I'm lost." The slight British accent he spoke with grew thicker by the second as he tried to conceal his anger.

"Look at it this way. You remember what happened to the last batch. We showed them things that would have been familiar to their previous selves."

"Yah, and it drove them over the edge."

"Yes, and what better test than to let them both be confronted with a place that would be more than familiar to their donors?"

"Yes. And see how they react."

"Correct. Why wait for them to flip out? Why not push them to it, if it's going to happen? Save ourselves the trouble later on. We only need them to be fine until we have a second generation. After that, they don't matter."

When Victor only stared in admiration, perhaps feeling a slight bit foolish, she continued, "And, if you've finished questioning my judgment, I'd like you to prepare things for his mate."

VII

Halfway through their conversation, Brian turned to his side, and saw people. They sat at tables, eating their meals as though the restaurant were back in business. To his left, in the water; ducks were swimming around, waiting for food from the dining tourists, as though most birds hadn't been wiped out of existence hundreds of years ago.

"Brian."

He turned back to George, startled, and everything was back the way it had been. The same abandoned restaurant, in a town empty of life.

"Sorry." He apologized.

"Thought I lost you there for a second."

"I thought I saw people... And Ducks."

"You're going to have to be careful of that."

"What do you mean?"

"Keep it under control. Remind yourself what's real. And most of all, don't let anyone back home know about it."

"But, *why*?" he asked, afraid for the first time today, remembering the fear he'd seen in Mary's eyes.

"There was another batch of clones before us."

"They gassed them, didn't they?" he asked, his eyes dropping to the table, not wanting to hear the answer.

"Yah, how'd you know?"

"I saw it, like I was there."

"Like you saw the people and the ducks."

"Yup."

"I'd like to drive you around. Show you some more things."

"Okay." He said greedily, eager to change the subject.

VIII

Victor Cycled the machine up, supposedly for a test run. He'd done this about a hundred times. The council had no idea.

After the first clones had been terminated, he'd been given the go ahead to re-collect the blood samples and then go back in time and eliminate the host's parents before they'd been born. He was given as much time to do it as it took him, but they wouldn't take no for an answer.

This, the council thought would eliminate the memories in the next set of subjects, because they would have no alternate life to remember. This ended up creating an alternate reality, where the subjects had never been born. The blood samples however, still existed somehow. They had no explanation for this, other than the possibility that the other timeline where they had been collected, still existed somewhere.

Victor had grown to like the murders. There were no consequences. Even if he did get arrested, he could merrily go along with the police; and when the timer went off back here, he'd be pulled back.

"Two hours should be enough." he said, and stood in the center of the eight foot ring." There was a crackle of energy, a tingling sensation and then cold dark nothing for a few seconds; and then he was there, shivering. His clothing stuck to his sweat-drenched body.

He reached for his gun. Caressed it with his left hand. His baby.

IX

"Shit!" Brian said, "*I used to live here*. In-fact at the age I am *now*, I would have still lived here with my parents."

"Don't you find that odd? That you remember it as though it's all happened *before* rather than remember it as it would be happening."

"You mean, as if I were this age in both times, and the future hadn't happened yet in either one?"

"Something like that. The guy I talked to said that was how the first clones remembered; as though it were still happening in both time-lines and they were experiencing each day from two perspectives."

"Why do you think we're different?"

"That's the part that scares me, and I try not to think about it."

"You think they went back and did something to silence the memories."

"That would seem the most likely answer."

"But if they went back and killed us, wouldn't that kill the memories?" he asked, "I mean, if there was suddenly no other life to remember, why do we remember it all here and now?"

"I don't know."

"The whole thing is so frustrating."

"Maybe that's one of the things that bothers Victor about you."

"What?"

"You don't sound like a seventeen year old, going on eighteen tomorrow."

"I don't think I did the first time around either."

X

Victor closed in on the man in the parking lot. He was about to kill Brian's father for the fifth time, when he had an idea.

Four times, he had killed the man. Four times, he'd done it a different way. But this time, he was going to let him live.

As long as he'd killed the man, things would not have changed. What he'd found was that when he went back to the exact moment he'd been in before, he ceased to be there as his previous self. So it was just one Victor, and he was able to live the whole thing over and over again, as many times as he liked.

Today, he decided, he would play before he killed him.

*

Brian stopped, eyes going wide. His heart was pounding. Something was wrong. They were walking across Madison Barracks now. An abandoned military base, which in Brian's time, had been rebuilt with military and civilian housing, restaurants, and some tourist attractions.

George stopped then. "Brian?"

"S ... Something's wrong."

"You don't look good at all."

'The year is two thousand and four and you are living in Watertown, New York.' his mind told him. Then, just as quickly, *'It's twenty six forty five, and you live at the North Country Research Foundation Community.'*

"Help." He said weakly, as his knees started to buckle and every muscle in his body seemed to give out at the same time, but he doubted his voice had been loud enough to hear.

Everything went gray.

*

Victor had gone next to July Fifteenth 2004. In minutes he would be closing in on Brian. Here he would be 28.

He watched as Brian closed in on his apartment building.

Letting him live would probably drive him nuts, but as far as the council would know, he was never born in this timeline.

"Hey, Brian." he shouted across the street.

Brian turned to face him, and was there a look of recognition? Fear, perhaps? He wondered then if it was affecting them in both timelines.

"What's wrong?" he asked, when he just stared at him.

"Do I *know* you?" he asked.

"Yah," he stated simply, reaching behind his back, "It's *me*, Victor."

*

George crouched over Brian's unconscious body.

His eyes opened suddenly, but he seemed to be in a trance, looking beyond everything here. "Do I *know* you?" he asked.

"Brian." George said, attempting to get his attention.

"Victor?" he asked, and seemed, despite his dazed state, to suddenly be afraid.

"No, *it's me*, George." he tried to comfort him.

*

Victor took his chance, while Brian seemed dazed, pulling the gun from the back of his pants, and put a bullet in his chest.

He only gave a startled gasp. Probably - Victor imagined - all he was capable of just then, and dropped.

Victor watched as the pool of blood formed beneath him for a few seconds, and then stooped down and grabbed his keys, which he'd been holding in his hands the whole time.

"There, you smart-ass, little shit!" he whispered.

"He shot me George." he wheezed, blood gurgling in his throat and trickling from his mouth, his eyes rolling up in his head.

This, Victor had not planned for, and he almost fell backward.

In this time-line, there was no George Castile.

He had been removed from existence.

'He shot me George.' A shiver slid down his spine.

He walked slowly to the house, knowing that he had plenty of time, and walked straight to the apartment on the third floor.

Here he collected a couple of souvenirs. One of which was an acoustic-electric guitar. *'This,'* he thought, *'will push him over the edge.'*

He played a little in the future, but seeing his guitar from a life that he never should have had... Now that would be fun to watch.

A smile slowly slid across Victor's face. With any luck, he'd get to be the one to terminate the fucker when he lost his little mind.

*

Brian looked pale.

"He shot me George," he wheezed, sounding as though he were having trouble breathing.

And then he just sat up straight.

"I'm dead." he said.

"No, you're alive," George stated firmly, concern in his voice. "You're in Twenty Six Forty Five. Look at me. It's George."

"George," he said, with what seemed like relief, "I knew I didn't just dream you."

"Brian, wake up." he shouted, shaking him now.

"Can't bro." he stated simply, "They want me now."

"Who wants you?" he asked, tears welling in his eyes.

"I don't know who they are. There's so much light, and they're calling for me."

"Jesus." he said. What could he say to this? Don't go into the light?

*

Now Victor was back in the parking lot, in 1975. A guitar strapped to his back. He pistol whipped the man from behind this time, and as he fell forward, he picked up his keys; A strong feeling of déjà vu came over him.

In a minute, he had the man on the back seat of his own car, and strangled the remaining life out of him.

He had an hour left.

It was time to have some fun. Sylvia was her name. And she was in the bar bathroom, freshening up so she could look her best.

No one noticed victor walking into the restroom.

None but Sylvia.

This was the second time he'd done this. He had taken her from behind, over the sink last time.

This time he told her to get on the floor.

As before, she told him he didn't need the gun, but as before, he held it to her head until he came in her, but instead of killing her this time, he let her live.

He looked at his watch for a moment, pulled her to a standing position.

"Want to see the eighth wonder of the world?"

She shook her head no.

Victor grabbed a fist-full of her hair, and pulled her over to one of the stalls; putting the gun away, and grabbing the guitar with his other hand, which he'd leaned against the wall.

She began to fight him now, thinking he was going to shoot her.

He turned her to him, and smiled, as a look of horror spread across her face, and then he let go of her, and everything brightened. He was back in the lab.

He was half tempted to go back and do it again, but decided against it.

*

Brian sat bolt upright.

"You okay now?" George asked.

"I don't think so." *'Of course you're not alright,'* he thought suddenly, *'You're dead ...'*

'Am not' he immediately argued.

"Hey, Brian. You still with me?"

"I think I know how they solved the dual memory problem."

*

Victor placed the guitar on Brian's bed, complete with a tag that said, *"From Victor."* If anyone asked why he had given it to him, he could simply say it was a wedding gift.

Just then, Veronica walked in.

"Have you seen Brian?"

"Umm," he blurted, at a complete loss now, "He'll be back in a little while."

She seemed unnerved suddenly, as though she might have seen something in his eyes that frightened her.

And very well, she should have, he thought just then.

Victor walked out quickly, without another word.

He had been tempted just then, and that wasn't good.

He had wanted her. Had wanted to do with her, what he'd done with women on his travels in time. Only thing was, that he couldn't set things back here. The machines would record temporal anomalies, and the council would know.

He was getting too used to being a god.

*

"Brian. Tell me what's going on." George pleaded.

"I think they killed us."

"What?"

"Yah, they killed us before we were old enough to know what had happened, so we would have no memories. But that wasn't enough for *him*."

"For *who*?" George asked, "You're talking crazy."

"He changes things. He goes back and plays."

George grabbed him this time and forced him to face him. "Who?"

"Victor." He grinned then, and something in Brian's eyes perhaps, seemed to unnerve his friend a bit. "He just killed me again. Only this time, he waited till I was older, maybe just to get back at me."

George had cold chills just then so strong that he shook noticeably, as a revelation hit him. "Or to try and push you over the edge."

"But why?" Brian asked, intrigued and frightened at the same time.

"The last batch of clones were terminated because they remembered and it drove them insane."

"Do you think he hates me that much?"

"I don't know. But no matter what happens, you have to make sure he doesn't find out that you know about it."

"But he won't stop, will he?"

"I don't know." he admitted, "Maybe if he doesn't think it's working."

XI

Brian walked into his room a few hours later, to find Veronica sitting on his bed with a Light tan colored acoustic-electric guitar in her hands.

His eyes instantly sought out and found a dent in the wood, at the bottom front of the instrument. It had happened when the strap lock broke on stage and he'd dropped it in another life.

The room started to spin and he had to grab the casing to keep from falling.

"Are you okay?" he heard Veronica ask from far away.

Taking slow, deep breaths he managed to right himself again, and walked to her. "I'm okay. Just tired."

"I'm Veronica," she said, smiling.

'I know,' he thought, but said, "Brian." and shook her hand.

Things were starting to make more sense than he wanted them to. Not only had they cloned *him*, but they had cloned all those who'd been close to him as well.

He picked up the guitar. An electrical current moved through his hands and up his arms, then surged through him, and he fought the urge to throw the instrument down.

He sat on the bed without thinking then, and started playing a song. One he had written in that other world, at the age of twenty two or so.

Veronica seemed a slight bit dazed, and took a couple of steps backward.

"Everything *okay*?" he asked her, setting the guitar on the bed. He'd written the song for her, and it seemed she was remembering.

She looked a bit confused as he neared her, and without thinking about it, he took her in his arms and kissed her on the lips. It was one of many kisses in his life, and his first at the same time. Something about that made it even more magical.

"How?" she asked.

"Just don't tell anyone." he said, holding her tight.

"So, you two are getting along well, I see." Victor said from the doorway. The look in his eyes was impossible to miss. He expected something. The guitar had been a part of his little game, and he'd wanted it to push Brian over the edge.

"Yes we are," Brian answered. "But you're quite the little *perv* now *aren't you?*"

"Wha ..." Victor began, startled for perhaps the first time that Brian had ever seen.

"Is that how you get your *kicks*? Watching kids make out?" Brian continued. He knew he needed to somehow get control of his anger, but he couldn't help it. In his head, he could see this man crossing the street... pulling a gun. *'It's me, Victor,'* he'd said right before pulling the trigger.

"Bry *don't*" Veronica interrupted.

"Oh, *Bry* is it?" Victor laughed. "She's got a *nickname* for you already. Why you'd think you were *married*.

Brian flashed to a marriage in his head, but brushed it off, and was able to keep his composure.

Veronica was not.

Victor noticed her reaction right away. "*Well, now*. Looks like all isn't right here *after all*." he said snidely and began walking into the room.

Brian didn't have time to think about what he was doing. He reached out quickly and grabbed a large, heavy wooden chair, lifted it above his head.

"What's wrong honey?" Victor asked, closing in on Veronica.

Brian brought the chair down hard into Victor's head, Lifted it again as he dropped to the floor, brought it down once more.

"Oh God!" Veronica exclaimed, looking as though she were going to be sick.

Brian quickly took the man's clearance card from a retractable clip on his belt, and removed a gun from the back of his pants, where he'd seen it on a few occasions.

"What are you doing?" Veronica asked.

XII

George had just entered the building and was about to go see Brian when the alarm went off.

A short ways ahead, Brian rounded the corner with a gun, and was telling a security guard to drop his weapon and back off.

The guard wasn't going to do it though, and George knew it. He had his gun trained on Brian.

George slowly closed the distance, carefully removing a fire extinguisher from the wall, and bashed the guard in the head with it.

He managed to squeeze off a shot as he went down, but luckily it missed.

George took off the man's belt, tying his hands together and to his legs, and pulled him into a supply closet.

"How do we get out of here?" Brian asked.

"We don't."

"What?"

"I found the time machine."

*

A few minutes later, with the alarms still going off around them, they stood in the time displacement chamber.

George ran to a console and typed something for a few seconds, and a large circular platform in the center of the room lit up.

He then walked over to them with two watches. "Put these on."

"What are they?"

"They're what's going to take you where you're going, but they'll also allow you to move through the time stream once you get there."

"What about you?"

"Right behind you."

Veronica hadn't said anything this whole time, and Brian was beginning to worry about her. "You okay?"

She nodded, "I guess I have to be."

Just then a guard burst into the room, and opened fire.

George pushed them into the center of the platform, and seconds later they were standing in a parking lot.

Veronica took hold of his arm, and the full weight of her almost knocked him over.

She said nothing, only looked at him, startled, and obviously in pain.

He took her in his arms, crouched down, noticing now the blood coming from her stomach.

She'd been shot before they could make it through. "I'll call 911." He assured her, but she was already slipping.

Rage filled him then, but there was nowhere to direct it.

She was gone a few seconds later.

He knew now that the emptiness he'd felt practically from birth, was just the feeling of being without her. Even though he hadn't realized it till now, he'd just been missing her from the other life.

And now he'd been given another chance with her, and he'd screwed it up.

'No.' he thought. *'He did.'*

As if on cue, a brief flicker of light marked the arrival of another traveler just a few yards away.

One who had been here many times.

Victor was so sure of his surroundings that he didn't even hear Brian approaching.

At the last second, he started to turn.

Brian Pistol whipped him in the face as he turned. Victor went down fast.

He took his gun, and pushed the other one right into his face.

"How did you ..."

"Shut up!" he screamed.

Brian held up a hand then. It still had fresh blood on it from Veronica.

"Know what *this is*?"

"They're going to erase you."

"This is *her* blood." With that he smeared it on Victor's face. "You *like that* ass hole?"

"What are you going to do?"

"Well," Brian said, fighting the urge to beat the man's face with the handgun until it was nothing but mush. "You took everything from me. It's only fair that I return the favor."

"Wait."

Brian smiled and pulled the trigger. His stomach threatened to turn, but he didn't throw up. He however hadn't anticipated how loud the sound of the gun would be.

Placing Victor's gun in the front waste of his jeans, he wiped his off, put it in Victor's hand.

"Hey!" some guy yelled from across the parking lot, closing on his position. "What's going on?"

Brian turned to face his father.

"This guy shot a woman and then himself. Call 911."

"Call *what*?"

"The *cops*." he said, realizing now that 911 probably didn't exist yet.

While the man was running toward the bar on the other side of the parking lot, he removed the watch from Victor's wrist and the one from Veronica, and placed them in his pocket. He then kissed veronica on the lips and pressed the button on the side of his watch.

It displayed a date and time. He adjusted it to read July fifteenth 2004.

Before he could press the button again though, a sharp pain tore through his skull.

He dropped to his knees, fighting the voices that threatened to drive him insane.

His mind argued that he was seventeen years old and living in Sackets Harbor, NY, and immediately yelled back that he was full of shit, attempting to iron out which reality was real. Except that they both were, and therein lied the problem.

He lifted the watch, needing something to happen ... Anything.

He pressed the button.

The voices stopped, as he arrived on the sidewalk across from his other self's apartment building.

XIII

George held off the guards as long as he could. He'd killed two of them already.

He just needed a couple more minutes. Hopefully Brian and Veronica did what they needed to do and were done.

This would trap them wherever they were.

The door blew inward then with great force and he found himself thrown to the ground.

Four guards rushed in just then and shot him before he could get to his feet.

He died knowing that he had at least removed the information on where the two had gone from the computer. It wouldn't take them long however, to track the watches and go to their location.

One of the guards moved quickly to the console, immediately noticing the bomb George had placed there.

They carefully removed it from the room, and as they reached the hallway, it went off.

If George had still been alive he would have been smiling.

The bomb was not only there to destroy the machine. It was a nice little toy he'd picked up from the lab which would release a virus into the air. A very fast acting one that would kill everything for miles.

XIV

Brian had made it to his apartment building minutes ago. The voices had blissfully silenced. He waited across the street to see himself get home to ensure that he'd done well.

Otherwise Victor might show to kill him again. After a half hour however, he realized that he wasn't going to see himself. If Victor was able to keep going to the same moment and killing the same people, then it must only be possible for one version of you to exist at the same instance in one timeline.

As this thought occurred to him, he realized why it was that he no longer heard the voices. Here, in this time, he was the only version of himself that existed. There was no conflict. Unless, of-course, he attempted to think of the past seventeen years. Then there were arguments, but those were ones he could handle. He looked down at his hands then, and realized that they had grown a slight bit.

He walked to the apartment building and looked at his reflection in the glass of the front door.

"Amazing." he remarked.

He had grown to the age his other self was in this time. He looked at his watch then, to see how much time he had, and realized that the numbers were changing rapidly.

Something was wrong.

He wasn't ready to be stuck here yet. As much as he wanted to run into the house and see if Veronica was there, he had other things to think of, and maybe only moments to do something.

He watched the dates cycle rapidly, until he saw one close to where he had come from in the future and he quickly pressed the button on the side of the watch. As he did though, the screen scrambled, and he only had a split second to panic before everything went white.

An instant later he was in the time displacement chamber.

Part of the building had collapsed and it appeared that he wouldn't be able to make it out of the room.

The machine looked to be intact, but there was no electricity.

The room was fairly well lit, despite the lack of power, as a section of the ceiling was missing and light from outside was pouring in.

The voices in his head started arguing immediately, but it was somewhat bearable. It was obvious now why the first group of kids had gone insane. What could he do though? Go back and kill his father again?

"Not an option." he told himself, when he realized that he had actually considered it for a moment. The only option was to go back and take over the life which had been stolen from him.

It was then that he realized the watch on his wrist was dead.

"Great."

He noticed A skeleton behind the desk on the floor then.

A few seconds later he had George's badge in his hand.

How was it possible that the body had been left here for so long?

Fifteen minutes later however, he had the answer to that.

*

Standing on the roof of the building, Brian could see for quite some distance.

There were bodies everywhere.

The whole colony looked to be dead.

"Did you do this George?"

All of these people were dead. Maybe they deserved it, but what of the clones? He guessed they couldn't have saved them all, and maybe this was the humane way to have handled it. Deep down, he wished there had been some other way.

"How was work?" Veronica asked.

"Oh not bad." he replied, and walked over to give her a kiss. "I missed you though."

Just as he leaned in, their lips almost pressed together, he snapped back just in time to keep from falling to his death from the roof.

"Jesus."

Something had to happen and quick, or he was going to lose his mind.

*

It had taken four hours to get power back up and running. Now that it was, he wasn't going to waste any time.

He had returned to the time displacement chamber and reprogrammed the machine to take him back in 30 seconds.

He thought about it for a few seconds, and wondered if he would be stealing his other self's life? What were the moral implications? His mind moved to Veronica then and he didn't care. It was his life damn it.

He thought of going back to the point in that timeline where he was seventeen, but he didn't want to live that part of his other life again. He remembered it well enough to know that.

As the final three seconds ticked by, Brian lit a stick of dynamite that he'd found while hunting around for power sources, and dropped it just before the machine relocated him.

The coordinates were still set to the hallway outside his apartment so that's where it took him.

As he arrived, the voice in his head stopped and his watch went dead.

Just then he thought he smelled smoke, and began to turn around as everything went white. It felt suddenly as though his body had been ripped apart, and just when he thought it would drive him insane, he was blessed by darkness.

XV

Brian awoke in a hospital bed.

He'd had one hell of a dream, but he couldn't remember what it was.

"Hey." Veronica said from a chair at his bedside.

"What happened?"

"You had a Seizure. The doctor said you'd be fine."

Brian only remembered a little bit of what had happened right before, but recent memories that he did have were confusing. It was like he was having a dual memory of the past. What he knew to be real, this reality, and what he knew had to be part of a dream.

"What's wrong?" Veronica asked noticing his quiet and perhaps the confused look on his face.

"Oh nothing. You ever have one of those dreams, where it seems when you wake up that you lived a whole other lifetime in there."

"Once or twice."

"I think that's all it was."

With the memory of this life feeling more and more solid by the moment, Brian was passing the future reality off as a lingering bad dream, and thinking about writing it down when he got home.

Then as they checked out, he was given his personal items in a bag.

He only needed to peek in once.

When he saw the watch, the whole thing came back to him.

Photo by Azure Lee. Digital work by Joseph Sweet.

Joseph Sweet was born in October of 1976. He's been writing since the age of Sixteen. Hell 101 is his first book, but there is much more coming.

He lives in Watertown NY. You can read more about him as well as his other projects at the website.

http://www.josephsweet.co.nr

www.ingramcontent.com/pod-product-compliance
Lightning Source LLC
Chambersburg PA
CBHW030816310726
48980CB00006B/519/J

* 9 7 8 0 6 1 5 1 6 3 8 7 1 *